The Master of Grex

Joan Wolf

Untreed
Reads

The Master of Grex
By Joan Wolf

Copyright 2020 by Joan Wolf
Cover Copyright 2020 by Untreed Reads Publishing
Cover Design by Ginny Glass

ISBN-13: 978-1-94913-551-0

Published by Untreed Reads, LLC
506 Kansas Street, San Francisco, CA 94107
www.untreedreads.com

Also available in ebook.

Printed in the United States of America.

Author's Note

Anne is based on a character in one of my favorite books, *The Duke's Children* by Anthony Trollope. In that book Lady Mabel Grex is in the same sad situation as Anne—she has a spendthrift father and brother who have stolen her dowry and let her house crumble down around her. Anne, however, is nicer than Lady Mabel, and, unlike poor Mabel, she has a happy ending. In tribute to Trollope I have kept the Grex name and the names of some of the characters in his wonderful novel.

The character of Daniel is loosely based on the life of the early nineteenth century social reformer, Robert Owen. Owen ran several factories in which he instituted the eight-hour day for his workers and saw to the education of their children. To the surprise of almost everyone (except Owen) his mills turned out to be quite profitable. Unfortunately, few other owners followed in his footsteps.

The most important English geologist of this period was William Smith who, in 1815 published the first geological map of Britain. He later published the Delineation of the Strata of England and Strata Identified by Organized Fossils. He is the man with whom Matthew is supposedly working.

The date for the action of this book is 1817, the year the Habeas Corpus Act was suspended, heavy taxes still lay on vital items such as tea, sugar, beer, soap and candles, and the Corn Laws still protected landowners and large farmers. It was also the year that Jane Austen died.

PART ONE
THE RETURN

CHAPTER ONE

Anne was brushing her beloved old mare's blood bay coat when Toby, the only groom left on the estate, came to tell her that her father had returned from London and wished to see her. She mustered up a smile and handed Molly's lead to Toby. "Take her back to her stall and make sure she has fresh water," she said.

"Of course, my lady." Toby, who had to be at least sixty, sounded injured.

Anne put her hand on his arm. "I'm sorry. I know you would never forget the water, Toby. I'm just a little...concerned at the moment. And not about Molly."

He gave her his toothless smile. "That's all right, my lady. I'll take good care of the princess here."

Anne flashed him a smile, then turned to walk across the paddock, past the stables and up the dirt road to the house. Her old governess, who had been with her since she was five, was waiting at the door. "He's in the library," she reported tersely. "Didn't look happy."

Percival's lost money at the races. The thought flashed instantly into Anne's brain. Her brother had been losing races ever since he went away to school. Granted, in Percival's case, the apple hadn't fallen far from the tree. Anne's father, the Earl of Grex, had been losing races for a lot longer than his son.

Anne moved gracefully down the hall to the small parlor, one of the few rooms on the ground floor that was still usable. She pushed open the door and saw her father standing in front of one of the tall windows, his back toward her. "You wished to see me, Papa?" she asked.

He swung around to face her. The Earl of Grex was a tall man with a red face and a well-established stomach. He was scowling. "There you are, Anne. Come in, come in, I must speak to you."

Anne walked into the room.

"Your brother has finished me," the earl said furiously. "On the very day that I won a considerable amount of money at Newmarket, what must he do but go and lose even more than I won! It cost me all my winnings and then some to pay his debt!"

"Well, why did you pay his debt, Papa?" Anne asked reasonably. "You must know he'll only bet on more horses."

The earl let out a long, exasperated breath. "Sit down, Anne. There are some matters we must discuss."

Anne complied, seating herself on a tattered velvet sofa. The earl sat across from her in a tired looking tapestry chair. "Percival and I had some dealings a few months ago that perhaps you should know about."

Anne was mystified. Her father never discussed any of his dealings with her; he only complained that he had no money.

"It has to do with the entail," Lord Grex said.

The fine lines of Anne's eyebrows drew together. Entails were legal documents that obliged a man's property, money, and title if he had one, to pass to his closest male heir. Which, in her father's case, was her brother Percival.

She said, "You cannot disinherit Percival, Papa. He is your legal heir."

"I know that." Anne's father glared at her. "If you would let me proceed…"

"I beg your pardon," Anne said softly. "I am listening."

"There is a clause in the entailment law that allows the entail to be broken if the heir—who must be of legal age—agrees to it."

Anne was stunned. She had known nothing of this. "Papa, did you make Percy agree to break the entail if you paid his gambling debts?"

The earl looked as embarrassed as it was possible for him to look. "No, he agreed to break the entail a few months ago if I would pay him a certain amount of money."

"And did you pay it?"

"Don't look at me like that, missy! It's paid now, that's for sure. Which means I can finally sell this crumbling old house and its useless property."

Sell Grex? Anne had few illusions about her father, but whatever may have been left of her esteem for him came crashing down with this news. She loved her home. It might be old and falling apart, but it was her home. It was where she felt safe.

"Mama is buried here! And Grandpapa and Grandmama, and all of their forebears going back hundreds and hundreds of years! You can't sell Grex, Papa!"

The earl looked at his daughter in a considering way. "If you care about it so much, I will give it to you for your dowry."

Anne looked at her father in utter bewilderment. "My dowry?"

"Yes. You are nineteen years of age and it's about time you got married. In fact, you must get married. I cannot afford to keep an unwed daughter. Just think—if I sell Grex, you'll have nowhere to go if you're not wed. I'm sorry, my dear, but the truth is, you've become a burden I can no longer afford."

The color drained from Anne's face. She and her father had never been close, but this felt like a punch in the stomach. To be told that she must marry herself out of his way because she was a burden! She tried to quell her rising distress and apply calm logic.

She said, "You have never put me in the way of meeting any eligible men, so I wonder at your dismay that I am still single."

"I know, I know. It's always my fault. But I have kept the town house in Berkeley Square for you. It will have to be sold, of course, but you can use it this spring to make your come-out. Perhaps it will be another inducement besides Grex. I'm afraid I shall have to use your dowry to pay for your come-out."

"You can't use my dowry! My mother left it to me for my marriage. You have no right to touch it."

"You will sign it over to me, missy, so I can pay for your damn come-out." He rose to his feet. "Now—I don't want to hear another unpleasant word. Go and huddle with that Miss Bonteen of yours.

5

She will tell you that I'm right. The only future for you, Anne, is to get married. And quickly!"

He stalked out of the room, his exit being made less dramatically effective by the stomach that caused him to waddle.

*

Anne rushed up the stairs and into the arms of her old governess.

"I heard his lordship's raised voice, my love," Miss Bonteen said worriedly. "Are you all right?"

Anne lifted her head. It was a little difficult to bury her face in Miss Bonteen's shoulder, as Anne was four inches taller. "I would like to kill him, Bonny," she said through her teeth. Her brown eyes blazed. "He is such a failure! A failure as a man, a failure as a noble, a failure as a Grex!" She unburdened herself to her dearest friend about everything her father had said.

Miss Bonteen sighed heavily. "I'm not surprised, my love. Your papa threw away his inheritance on the horses, and your brother followed in his footsteps. That's why you didn't make your come-out last year, as you should have. There was no money."

Anne looked into the clear hazel eyes of the only mother she had ever known; her birth mother having died when she was but four. "He said I could have Grex as my dowry. Perhaps there is a chance that we can stay here."

"Oh Anne. It would cost a fortune to put Grex into livable shape. I doubt there are many men who would spend their money on a falling down house in Yorkshire."

"I hate him!" Anne said with passion. "And I hate Percival too!"

"Hate is a very strong word, my dear."

"I know. Strong and accurate."

Miss Bonteen gave her a stern look. "You have been brought up to be a Christian woman, Anne Saxton. I don't ever want to hear talk like that coming from your mouth."

Anne sighed, some of the anger dissipating, as it always did when Miss Bonteen spoke to her in that tone of voice. "I'm sorry, Bonny," she said. They both moved toward the small sofa that stood in front of Anne's fireplace. "I'm curious about one thing, though," Anne said as they sat beside each other on the old chintz sofa.

"What is that, my love?"

"Where is Papa going to find a lady to launch this come-out he is so set upon? I must have a sponsor."

"Don't you worry, my dear. His lordship will find you a sponsor. Of that I am quite certain."

Anne sighed. "I wouldn't mind a chance to go to balls and the theatre and the opera. And I've always thought I would marry." She sighed again.

She sounded so gloomy that Miss Bonteen picked up her hand and squeezed it. Anne turned to her and smiled. "No one is going to want to marry me, Bonny. The only dowry I have is Grex, and who will want that? I love it, it's part of who I am, but no sensible man would want to encumber himself with such a falling-down wreck."

"I've never said this to you, Anne, because I didn't want to turn your head, but you've turned into a beautiful young woman. Some man will fall in love with you and marry you and give you babies. I'm sure of it."

Anne smiled again and shook her head. "Dearest Bonny, you always try to make me feel better."

Miss Bonteen smiled back and patted her hand.

*

Miss Bonteen had been correct about the earl's ability to find a sponsor and chaperone for his daughter—he produced a cousin from his deceased wife's side of the family, the Luptons. Cousin Julia had married an earl and presented him with five sons but no daughters, and she would be delighted to take Anne under her wing.

7

"Very high *ton*," Lord Grex told Anne. "Julia knows everyone who matters. She'll see to it you get to all the proper balls. And to Almack's, of course."

"I don't believe I've ever met Cousin Julia," Anne said. Father and daughter were standing on the back lawn of Grex House where Anne had been throwing a ball for her spaniel. Anne pushed a lock of hair that had come loose from its tie off her face, and gave the ball to Dorothy to hold in her mouth.

"She's a cousin of your mother's," Lord Grex said. "I haven't had much to do with that family since your mother died. They're so respectable they make me want to puke."

Anne had an idea that it wasn't her father who had broken the connection. Lord Grex's lamentable lifestyle would put off any respectable family.

"Your cousin said you could reside at her London house," Lord Grex continued. He smiled with satisfaction. "Thank God. Now I won't have to open the house in Berkeley Square."

"That should save you some money, Papa," Anne said, her tone of voice distinctly acidic.

He gave her a long stare. She stared back. This duel was broken by the spaniel who dropped the ball and sneezed on the earl's polished boots. Lord Grex swore and raised his foot as if to kick the dog.

Anne snatched the spaniel up into her arms. "Don't take out your bad temper on my dog, Papa!"

Lord Grex muttered a curse under his breath. "That dog's a menace. It's because you spoil her. Dogs need discipline, Anne. You must remember that."

"Dogs need love, Papa. All living creatures need love."

"I have no time for love just at the moment, Daughter. I need money. A great deal of money. If I can get you off my hands, sell the London House—and maybe even Grex itself—then I shall have time for all the love in the world." He gave her one last stare, turned on his heel and walked away.

Anne watched her father's retreating back and tried to stifle the fury that was running through her veins. She had always vaguely disliked her father, but until now she had never held him in contempt. The spaniel wiggled in her arms and she bent to put the dog down. "I don't know who he thinks will marry me," she said to Dorothy, who was assiduously sniffing the grass. "I have no dowry. Of course, strictly speaking, I suppose that's not true—he's going to offer Grex as my dowry. I expect he thinks there will be men lining up to be the owner of this ruined estate." She sniffled and swallowed hard. "But I love Grex, Dorothy. Our family is one of the oldest in Great Britain—there are records that show that."

Dorothy looked up and wagged her tail in joyous agreement.

Anne laughed and brushed away the few teardrops that had slid down her cheeks. "Come along, sweetie. We'll go to the stable to see Molly. Maybe we'll even go for a ride. Would you like that?"

The spaniel knew the word ride and gave an eager bark. "Come along, then, let's go." Anne crossed the lawn and turned right to take the road that led to the stable.

*

Unlike Anne, Miss Bonteen was ecstatic that her charge would be going to London to make her come-out into society. "Lady Moresack is one of London's great hostesses, my love. If she is to sponsor you, you will go to all the greatest balls—and you'll be assured of an entrée to Almack's."

Anne smiled at her governess-turned-companion. "I suppose you know about Lady Moresack from all the on-dits you read in the newspaper."

Living as they did in the "wilds of Lancastershire" as Miss Bonteen would say, the *Post* came to them a day late. This didn't disturb Miss Bonteen, however. Since Waterloo had ended the war against Napoleon, her chief interest was the goings-on of the upper class. Anne hardly read the paper at all. She preferred the books in the Grex library.

The invitation to join Lady Moresack in London came a week after Anne's conversation with her father. The Countess wrote she was "so looking forward to meeting Anna's little girl." As she had no daughters of her own, she would regard Anne as an adopted daughter and 'move heaven and earth' to find her a husband."

"It must really be bad if Lady Moresack thinks she will have to move heaven and earth to get me married," Anne said gloomily to Miss Bonteen as they sat at the breakfast table with the butter-stained letter they had passed back and forth.

Miss Bonteen said firmly, "Do not be such a pessimist, Anne. You are a beautiful young lady. You come from one of the oldest families in Great Britain. Not every gentleman is fixated on the amount of one's dowry. With Lady Moresack to stand behind you, I am sure you will have more offers than you know what to do with."

Bonny was trying so hard to cheer her up that Anne elected not to disagree. She looked into her companion's lovely eyes and smiled. "You're right, Bonny. I must be more optimistic. Perhaps there will be a prince for me in London."

Miss Bonteen smiled back. "That's better. That's how I like to hear you sound. Now, be sure to keep me apprised of how you go on. I shall be looking for a letter every day."

Anne put down the piece of toast she was about to bite into. "You won't need to wait for a letter, Bonny. You're coming with me."

Miss Bonteen dropped her eyes to her plate. "My dearest girl," her voice was very gentle, "Lady Moresack will have her own servants. She won't need me."

There was a long silence, and when finally Miss Bonteen looked up from her plate, Anne said slowly and clearly, "You are not a servant, you are my dearest friend. I will not go if you won't go with me. If Lady Moresack doesn't have a room for you, you can sleep in mine."

"My darling, it won't be for you to decide this question."

"Yes, it will be. And I never want to hear you call yourself a servant again. You are the only mother I've ever had and I'll be...damned...if I'm going to leave you at home."

Tears began to run down Miss Bonteen's smooth cheeks. "I shall treasure those words forever, Anne. Thank you."

Anne pushed her chair back and went over to give her friend a hug. "I love you and I won't have you diminished—not even by yourself. Is that clear?"

Miss Bonteen looked up into the young face of the girl she loved more than anything in the world. "Yes," she said. "It's perfectly clear."

CHAPTER TWO

The trip from Yorkshire to London was a long one. Anne didn't mind, she liked looking out the coach window at the changing scenery, but Miss Bonteen—who was 45, not 19, and who suffered from motion sickness—found the trip exhausting. Anne, apprehensive about her proposed London stay, wished the trip would last longer. Miss Bonteen felt very much the opposite, and was extremely relieved when their carriage finally came to rest in a large garden square with four sides of elegant town houses surrounding it. Anne put her arm around Miss Bonteen as a footman came down the front steps with a stool so they could alight.

"We're here, Bonny," she said encouragingly. "You'll feel better once you have some tea."

The coach door opened and Miss Bonteen alighted in a less than graceful fashion. Anne followed and the two women followed the footman up to the front door, where a butler was standing to greet them.

"I'm afraid Lady Moresack is not here to greet you, my lady," he said to Anne, his voice a deep rumble. "We did not know the precise time of your arrival and she has gone out. I will send for Mrs. Cole, the housekeeper, and she will show you to your rooms."

"Thank you," Anne replied in her clear young voice. "My companion, Miss Bonteen, is feeling ill from the long ride. Would it be possible to have some tea sent up to her?"

"Of course, my lady. I will arrange it."

In due course the housekeeper arrived, and the two newcomers passed through the large hall to the staircase and thence to the upper floors where their rooms were located. "We have put you in the yellow room, my lady," Mrs. Cole said. "Miss Bonteen has the room beside it."

"I would like to see Miss Bonteen made comfortable first, Mrs. Cole," Anne said. "She is not a good traveler and we have come all the way from Yorkshire."

Mrs. Cole took charge and Anne was relieved to see her friend tucked up with a cup of tea at hand should she want one.

Anne's own room was pretty, with a white painted fireplace and a thick Persian rug on the floor. Everything looked so well kept. It made Anne realize more sharply how dilapidated her own home had become.

A maid came in to unpack Anne's bags, and she stood at the window while the girl worked, surveying the houses that were grouped around the central garden. They were substantial dwellings, many of them built of brown brick with red dressings. The afternoon light was pouring in through Anne's bedroom window and the gated garden was greening in the early spring weather. Anne smiled at the garden. She was excited to be in London, but she would miss springtime in the country.

When the maid had finished, Anne thanked her. She was just planning to step next door to see how Miss Bonteen was faring when a light knock came upon her door. It opened to reveal a well-dressed woman who said, "May I come in? I'm your Aunt Julia!"

Anne smiled warmly. "Of course you can come in!"

The countess not only came in, she opened her arms and Anne, after a brief hesitation, went to be hugged. The countess was smaller than Anne, and she smelled divine. When she allowed Anne to step back, she looked up at her and clapped her hands. "But you're lovely! That will make my job easier."

Anne didn't know how to answer, so she simply smiled and said, "Thank you, my lady, for your great kindness to me."

"Tut, tut," her mother's cousin said. "I am delighted to have a daughter, even if she is borrowed. And I was very fond of your mother." She tilted her head. "You have her eyes—those great dark, long-lashed eyes we were all so jealous of when we were young."

Anne, who had no memory of her mother, was delighted to hear her being spoken of with such familiarity. "I didn't know she had brown eyes, my lady. My father doesn't ever speak of her, and she never had a portrait painted."

"Your father." Lady Moresack pinched up her mouth. "Well, never mind. You must come downstairs and take tea with me. And please call me 'Aunt Julia'." She gave a little skip and smiled. "I am so happy to have you here, Anne. We are going to have such fun!"

*

The following week flew by as Aunt Julia took Anne on a whirlwind shopping trip up and down Bond Street. Anne hadn't been surprised when her aunt proclaimed the clothes she had brought with her to be totally unsuitable for London. She was stunned, however, when she saw the exorbitant prices that were being asked for the new dresses, hats, gloves, shoes, shawls, riding habit, etc. She hoped her father was paying for some of this, that it was not all coming out of Aunt Julia's purse. She assuaged her guilt by telling herself it was her dowry money that was paying for all this, not Aunt Julia.

Anne's first introduction to London society would be at a ball given by Lord and Lady Althorpe. "Maria Althorpe is a friend of mine," Lady Moresack said with obvious pride. "She is very high in the instep, you know, but when I asked her if I could bring you, she was charmingly accommodating."

Anne had not met many ladies of fashion in her young life. In fact, she had never met any, and the coming ball was making her nervous. Miss Bonteen had taken her to a few assemblies in the local village, but that was the extent of her dancing experience. She greatly feared she wouldn't measure up to the standard of Lady Althorpe. And what if no one asked her to dance?

That particular fear was relieved when Lady Moresack's youngest son, Jeremy, paid a visit to his mother. He had come down from Oxford only last year, and he lived in some pleasant rooms that looked onto St. James Park. He had groaned when his mother told him she expected him to attend the Althorpe ball, but when he met Anne he changed his mind. He thought she was very pretty and very nice, and he assured her he'd dance with her and would find some other fellows to dance with her as well.

*

On the evening of the ball Anne stood looking into the pier glass mirror in her bedroom hardly believing what she saw. She looked elegant. She looked sophisticated. She looked like she might even belong at a London ball. Her dress was simple and graceful, a pale blue gauze worn over an underdress of white satin. Her mass of dark hair was gathered into a high knot with strands curling on her long neck. Aunt Julia had lent her a pearl necklace and earrings (Anne's father had sold all her mother's jewelry long ago), and she wore soft little slippers to match the dress.

I look so much older, she thought, as she gazed at this new self. She was accustomed to wearing riding clothes and old frocks. The few dinner dresses she owned were childish compared with the elegant gown she was wearing now. And when she came down the stairs, and Jeremy looked up and exclaimed, "You look beautiful, cuz!" she thought, for the first time since her father proposed this mad scheme, that perhaps someone might marry her after all.

*

There was a line of carriages several blocks long waiting to get into the Althorpes' townhouse, and the closer they got the more amazed Anne became. When they finally stepped into the front hall, taking their places in line to go upstairs to be greeted by their host and hostess, her eyes widened at the magnificence of the women around her. The satins and silks, the diamonds and rubies and sapphires, the elegantly curled hair…it was overwhelming for a girl who had been brought up at Grex.

To maintain her confidence Anne reminded herself that none of these people came from so old or distinguished a family as hers. She owed it to her ancestors to put on a brave face, and when Lady Moresack introduced her to Lady Althorpe, Anne smiled naturally and dipped into a graceful curtsy.

"So pretty," the Vicountess murmured to her aunt.

"Thank you," Aunt Julia replied.

Jeremy passed through the line after them, and then they were at the ballroom door. Anne halted at the top of the three marble steps that led down to the polished wood floor and looked around. The orchestra was seated opposite to the stairs, and every bit of space that was not taken up by the dance floor was filled with people. "Anthea's invitations are never refused," Aunt Julia said into her ear, "All the most distinguished members of the *ton* are here tonight."

"And still more are coming," Anne said, glancing toward the crowd that had been behind them in line.

Aunt Julia put her hand on Anne's elbow and steered her down the stairs. "Come along. I see some people I want to introduce you to."

It was about halfway through the evening, and Anne was standing with Jeremy, his friend Martin Abbey and Martin's sister Margaret. They were all a little flushed from dancing and they were sipping champagne, a beverage Anne had never tasted before. She had enough sense not to tell the others such a thing, though, and wrinkled her nose a little at the bubbles. She didn't like it, but she wasn't going to say that either.

"Do you like to ride?" Margaret Abbey asked Anne. "It's very fashionable to be seen in Hyde Park in the late afternoon. It might be fun to get up a small party."

Anne thought of her beloved old mare left at home. "I love to ride, but I don't have a mount here in London."

"You could ride my mother's horse," Jeremy said. "He's a grand old fellow and she hardly ever takes him out. She prefers to drive."

"I couldn't possibly take your mother's horse." Anne spoke with astonishment that he should even think such a thing. She would never dream of allowing an unknown person to ride her precious Molly. And in the city! She said, "For all you know, I could be a dreadful rider who would bang on his back and hang on his mouth."

"Are you a dreadful rider?" Jeremy asked.

"Of course I'm not," she snapped. "But you only have my word for it."

Jeremy was opening his mouth to reply when a ripple of interest went around the ballroom. Anne noticed that people were looking toward the stairs, and she turned to see what was drawing so much attention.

A slender, black-haired man stood on the top step, his eyes sweeping the room as if he were a general assessing a battlefield. "Who is that?" Anne asked Jeremy in a lowered voice.

"It's Daniel Dereham," Jeremy replied in a whisper. "What is he doing here?"

"I thought he was up north building a factory," Martin said, his voice lowered as well.

"But what can he be doing here?" Jeremy said. "Lady Althorpe, of all people, would never allow anyone like him inside her kitchen let alone her ballroom."

"Yes, but Lord Althorpe is one of the leaders of the Whigs in parliament," Martin said. "He and a few other men have been pushing for social reform for the poor. Apparently Dereham is going to pay more money for fewer hours of work than other cotton mills, and the Manchester mill owners are furious. My father says a factory like that is only going to contribute to the general social unrest in the country. But men like Althorpe and some of the other Whigs in parliament are supporting Dereham's ideas."

Lord Althorpe had joined the young man at the top of the stairs, and now the two were coming down onto the ballroom floor. They halted under a chandelier, the newcomer's black hair glinting under the lights. As Anne watched, several other men began to gravitate in the direction of the new arrival. Lady Althorpe stepped up beside her husband, and, her back rigid with disapproval, gave Dereham her hand.

"Lady Althorpe looks as if touching him is some sort of torture," Anne said.

"He's not one of us," Jeremy said. "He's one of those nabobs who went out to India and came home with a fortune. There are all sorts of wild stories about how he became so rich, but no one knows for sure. He's a bit of a mystery."

"Goodness," Anne said.

The music started up again, and Martin asked Anne to dance.

CHAPTER THREE

Anne saw the famous—or infamous—Daniel Dereham again two days after the ball when she was riding in the park. It was just after sunrise and she and Jeremy were galloping along under the trees, something that was not allowed during the afternoon fashion parade. Anne was just about to pull up, when her horse stumbled and went lame on his right fore. She jumped off and bent down to pick up the horse's foot. Just as she had suspected, there was a stone wedged under Oliver's shoe.

Jeremy joined her, looking down at the hoof Anne was holding. He made a face and said, "That looks like it's in there pretty good."

"Do you have a hoof pick with you?" Anne asked.

"No. Do you?"

"No. The paths are so well groomed I didn't think I'd need one."

"Let me see if I can push it out," Jeremy said. "Hold Sedgwick, will you, Anne?"

She took his horse's reins and watched as Jeremy tried to move the stone. Oliver stood on three feet with his head hanging down. Anne stroked his neck with the hand that wasn't holding reins. Neither of them heard the approach of another horse until it was almost on them. Anne's head jerked around as a gleaming black horse pulled up next to them. A voice said, "Do you need help?"

"Do you have a hoof pick with you?" Anne asked urgently. "My horse has a stone in his shoe and we can't get it out."

"I have a knife." The horseman swung down from his saddle and removed something from a pocket. As he opened the knife, Anne moved back to make way for him and Jeremy held the reins. The man knelt and lifted Oliver's leg. "Now how did that get in there, eh boy?" he said in a gentle voice, as he fitted the knife under the stone and levered it out. He returned Oliver's leg to the ground, the horse tested it gingerly, then put his weight on it again.

21

"Thank you so much," Anne said gratefully. "When I'm home I always carry a pick, but I didn't think I'd need one in this well-maintained park."

"If there's trouble to be got into, you can always count on a horse to find it," the man replied in a voice that had a faint lilt to it.

"Too true," Anne said, and for the first time really looked at their rescuer.

Daniel Dereham had a beautiful face, with chiseled cheekbones, a straight nose, and light blue eyes that held the crystalline quality of a spring sky. An amused expression flickered across that face, and Anne realized she was staring. "Sorry," she apologized. "I didn't mean to stare." She added, "But I suppose you're used to it by now."

The amused expression turned into a smile. He didn't answer.

Jeremy said, "You were a life saver Mr. Dereham, and Oliver thanks you as much as we do. I've never had that happen in the park before."

"There are stones everywhere in life," Daniel Dereham returned. "I've found it's well to remember that." He turned to his own horse, threw the reins back over his neck and swung into the saddle. For the first time Anne looked at his horse and her eyes widened. "Is he an Arabian?" she asked.

"He is. Now, if you will excuse us, we'll continue with our ride."

Anne and Jeremy stood on the path and watched as the Arabian exploded into a full gallop. In a moment man and horse had disappeared from sight.

"That was Daniel Dereham," Jeremy said blankly.

"So you said," Anne replied.

"He's....he's..." Jeremy ran out of words.

"He's stunning," Anne said.

Jeremy grinned at her. "You held your own, Anne. I couldn't find a thing to say."

She laughed. "We didn't exactly have a conversation. But the man can't be a bad person. He stopped to help Oliver, and he rides like an angel."

"I never said he was bad," Jeremy protested.

"You said he wasn't one of us."

"Well, he's not. Actually no one seems to know very much about him, other than he made a fortune in India. Where he came from, who his parents were…no one seems to know. He just appeared on the scene last year and immediately went to work building this cotton factory in Lancashire. He's a mystery."

Oliver pushed his nose against Anne's arm and she turned to stroke his neck. "I think I'll hand-walk him home," she said. "He probably bruised his foot and it's best not to add any weight."

"Nonsense," Jeremy said. "I'll walk him and you can ride Sedgwick."

"I'm not dressed to ride astride," Anne gently pointed out to her cousin.

Jeremy's lips tightened and his cheeks flushed. Anne realized that it would embarrass him to ride while she walked, and she said, "We can both hand-walk our horses."

Her cousin's flush subsided, he agreed and the both of them started down the path that would take them home.

*

A few weeks went by and Anne's father arrived unexpectedly in London. He had been staying with friends at Newmarket, but the horses had not come in for him, and he thought it was time to take a break and check on his daughter. Lord Grex dropped off his baggage at the Clarendon Hotel, where he would have the freedom to come and go as he pleased. He planned to spend his evening at Brooks, where there was always a good game of cards, and tomorrow he would see how his daughter was faring in her quest for a husband.

Accordingly, Lord Grex called at Grosvenor Square the following morning, and was pleased when Lady Moresack's butler told him that Lady Anne was receiving a few friends in the blue salon. "Good, good," he said cheerfully. "Glad to hear the girl has made some friends. I'll just pop along to say hello." Leaving the butler behind, he strode down the corridor toward the sound of voices and stopped in the doorway to appraise the scene before him.

Three young men sat around Anne, who was looking lovely in her new blue muslin morning dress. There was another girl in the room, but Lord Grex didn't think she held a candle to Anne.

Lady Moresack saw him first and rose to greet him. Lord Grex smiled and motioned her out into the hallway. "Who are these chaps?" he asked.

"One is Mr. Ellery, the grandson of Lord Castleton, one is Mr. Abbey, who comes from an excellent family, and one is Lord Henry Melton, third son of the Duke of Sandcross. They all seem very taken with Anne."

"Do they have money?" Lord Grex asked bluntly.

Lady Moresack looked offended. "They all have decent incomes, Grex. I wouldn't have encouraged them if they hadn't."

The earl did not look happy. He had been hoping for more than a decent income. He told this to Lady Moresack.

A flush mounted to her cheeks. "Considering that Anne has no dowry, and that her father and brother have gambled away the family fortune, I think you should be grateful to see your daughter placed with a man who is fond of her and can give her a comfortable home. She is a lovely girl and I have grown quite fond of her."

Lord Grex knew when to retire from the field of battle and he made his way out of the house and back into the square without bothering to speak to his daughter. On the spur of the moment, he decided to check out of Clarendon's and head back to Newmarket, where he had friends who appreciated him.

*

While Lord Grex was visiting in Grosvenor Square another sort of meeting was going on, not in Mayfair but in the city. Mr. James Adams of Barings Bank was meeting with one of his largest accounts. When Daniel Dereham returned from India, he had taken out two safe boxes in Mr. Adams' bank, in which he had deposited a fortune in jewels. This was the first time he had requested a meeting with Mr. Adams, and Adams was nervous. The bank had facilitated the sale of two of Dereham's magnificent jewels, the proceeds of which he was using to build a manufacturing facility for cotton in Lancashire.

As the young man came into his office, Adams rose to greet him. After the handshakes and the offer and refusal of tea, he asked, "What can I do for you, Mr. Dereham? How is the factory coming along?"

"It's built," Dereham said. "All I need to do now to finish the project is to build cottages for the workers to live in."

This was the first Adams had heard about workers' cottages. "Cottages?" he queried. "I did not know you planned to build cottages."

"I want my workers living close to the factory," Dereham said.

"Oh. Well, I suppose that makes sense," Adams said.

"I have a few questions for you, Adams, in regard to the companies you would recommend I use for furniture and other household items. I can't just put in rugs and a few tables, as I would in India. The English like to surround themselves with more things."

Mr. Adams gave a nervous laugh. He was forty-six, twenty years older than the man in front of him, but there was something about Daniel Dereham that was intimidating. His idea of building a single factory, and not have his employees work from their home cottages, was still somewhat revolutionary in the cotton business. And no one had thought to build housing for their workers. That was unheard of.

The two men finished their discussion within half an hour, and Dereham hadn't been gone three minutes before Adams' next-door neighbor, James Brines, came in the door. "What did he want?" he demanded, taking the seat just vacated by the subject of his inquiry.

"He told me the factory building is completed and now he wants to put up cottages for the workers to live in. He was asking me for the names of companies that deal in furnishings."

"The factory is finished? That was fast."

"He was on the premises the entire time it was going up. I don't imagine there was much slacking off."

"He's a strange one." Brines shook his head. "With all that money, you'd think he'd hire people to oversee things for him. I can't imagine any of our other clients sitting in the wilds of Lancashire to watch a building go up."

"He's not the sort of man one asks about his behavior," Adams said dryly.

Brines leaned closer. "The rumor going round is that he's the bastard son of some great lord."

"I've heard that as well. All I can tell you is that he's richer than any of the great lords we have banking with us. I've never seen such jewels as those he packed into the safe boxes."

"I'd go out to India myself if I thought I could be the tiniest bit as successful as he was," Brines said.

"Who wouldn't?" Adams said.

Both men laughed. Brines went back to his office and Adams returned to work.

CHAPTER FOUR

Because of his presence at Lady Althorpe's ball, Daniel was invited to social events in homes that otherwise would never have been open to him. The thinking clearly was: if he's good enough for the Althorpes, he's good enough for us. And he has all that money.

To the irritation of the ladies, who were not unmoved by his beauty, Daniel did not use his sudden acceptability to grace the dance floor. Instead he passed his time in the card room, evaluating the usefulness of the men who invariably inhabited this space. Now that the factory was almost finished, he was ready to begin on the next phase of his grand plan.

He finally settled on Lord Neviss as being his best bet. Neviss was a pleasant man in his early forties whose younger brother had gone out to India about the same time as Daniel. Consequently, Neviss knew more about Daniel's Indian career than any of the other men in London, and he had kept quiet about it. Daniel appreciated this, and decided he was a man to trust. So he invited Lord Neviss to join him one afternoon in the suite of rooms he had hired at the Pulteney Hotel in Piccadilly.

"I gather you've come home to stay, then?" Lord Neviss asked, as the two of them sat in Daniel's large three-room suite sipping the hotel's fine brandy.

"Yes. India was an experience I shall never regret, but when the Maharajah's eldest son made it clear that I would be wise to leave while my heart was still beating, I decided to take his advice."

"Got too chummy with his Papa, eh?"

Daniel shrugged. "It seems he thought that way. I managed to get out with most of my assets and took ship for home."

"And now that you're here, what are your plans? I understand you've built a cotton mill in Lancashire."

Daniel gave a wry smile. "I have, and it seems to have caused a great deal of notice."

Lord Neviss simply said, "You're a man with a great deal of money. Of course people are interested in you."

Daniel put his glass down. "What I want to do now is buy a house. An historic house that has land."

Lord Neviss regarded the younger man with surprise. This was not an answer he had expected. He weighed what he should say next, then decided to be honest. "There is gossip going around that you are the bastard son of an English nobleman. Are you aware of that?"

Two level black eyebrows lifted. "How did a rumor like that get started?" The flexible voice was suddenly chilly.

Lord Neviss shrugged. "How does any rumor get started? Someone hears something from someone and passes it on, and soon it takes on a life of his own."

What Neviss did not say was that Daniel Dereham's face shouted his heritage. There was only one nobleman in Britain who had black hair and black lashed crystalline blue eyes that were identical to the ones of the young man sitting across from him.

"I am not interested in discussing my parentage." The voice now was cold and dismissive. "I am my own man."

"If you are your own man, why not just build a grand house that will be your own? Why does it have to be an historic house?"

"I like history," came the brief reply.

"Hmmm." Lord Neviss took a sip of his excellent brandy.

Daniel was silent and Lord Neviss regarded him with respect. This was not a lad who was easily plumbed. He said, "Do you have plans to marry as well?"

"Eventually, yes. Once I have my estate I shall want an heir."

Lord Neviss appreciated that he was being taken into a close-held confidence. The boy was serious. Very serious. And he wasn't placed to know what he needed to know, which is why he was asking for Lord Neviss' help. For this reason, his lordship felt flattered.

"The difficulty with finding an historic home and property for sale is that such estates are almost always entailed," he explained. "An entail insures that by law the property must go to the nearest male heir in order that it will never pass out of the family. Consequently, even owners who are desperate for money are unable to sell their property assets, however much they may wish to do so."

"I understand that," Daniel said. "But I would be most appreciative if you would be kind enough to inform me should something become available."

"Do you have any preference for location?"

"The north would be best, but I understand I can't afford to be choosy."

There was something about this young man that told Lord Neviss he usually got what he wanted. So instead of discouraging him, Lord Neviss said that he would be happy to keep his ears open.

The two men finished their brandies and parted with mutual good will.

*

Anne, who had lived like a hermit at home, began by enjoying the social life in London. But after a month of balls and musicales and routs and breakfasts and stately rides in Hyde Park at five in the afternoon, city life had begun to pall. She didn't like the dirt of London. She didn't like the ragged children she saw everywhere, begging for money, sweeping horse manure from the streets when they should be home with a family. The majesty of the opera dimmed when she stepped outside and was confronted with desperate girls trying to sell her flowers. And London smelled bad. She found herself longing for the fresh, clean air of the countryside.

In short, Anne was homesick. She missed Grex. She missed her mare and her dog and all her favorite haunts on the property. More than anything else, she missed the quiet.

Aunt Julia kept telling her that one or the other of her "suitors" would come up to scratch, but so far none of them had. Aunt Julia never said, but Anne knew from Jeremy, that the families of her various beaux were not happy about a match with a penniless girl, no matter how ancient her pedigree.

"You just have to stay the course, Anne," Jeremy said to her early one morning, as they rode through Hyde Park. "I know for certain that Abbey is working on his papa. And Margaret is helping. Martin really cares for you, you know."

A squirrel dashed across their path and Oliver threw up his head. Anne patted him reassuringly and said, "Martin talks about his parents' house in Sussex quite often. If I married him would I live there? It sounds as if it's very pretty."

This was not a question Jeremy had considered. "Don't know, Anne. Why don't you ask him?"

Anne said with exasperation, "Jeremy, I can't ask a man who hasn't proposed to me where I would live if I married him!"

"I suppose not," Jeremy conceded grudgingly.

They had been walking their horses during this discussion and now the drum of galloping hooves sounded behind them. They moved their horses to the side of the path and watched as a black horse shot by, churning the dirt of the path in his wake. Anne's horse was startled and reared. She brought him down, once more patted his neck, and said to Jeremy, "Oliver is a little spooky today. Why don't we walk quietly until he settles down?"

They moved back to the middle of the path and were preparing to ride on when they saw the black horse returning at a trot. The rider pulled up in front of them and said to Anne in a pleasant tenor voice, "I apologize for blowing past you like that. We usually ride earlier, and I'm accustomed to having the park to myself. I didn't mean to startle your horse. Is everything all right?"

Anne had recognized Daniel Dereham when he passed them, and she replied calmly, "Oliver was a little spooked, but everything is fine."

"Well," he repeated, "My apologies."

Anne said, "Your horse is gorgeous."

"Thank you."

"Our thoroughbreds are beautiful creatures, but there's something about that Arabian face I just love. It's so...so..."

"Intelligent?" Daniel said.

She smiled. "Perhaps that's it."

He glanced at the sky. "I must be getting back. Again, apologies for my rudeness." He didn't seem to move at all, but the Arabian instantly set off at a ground-covering trot.

"Well," Jeremy said, as he watched the figure disappear from sight. "That's twice we've met him in the park, and twice I didn't say a word."

"Did you want to say something?" Anne inquired.

"I did."

"What did you want to say?"

"I don't know."

Anne started to laugh.

"There's something daunting about that fellow," Jeremy complained. "I don't know exactly what it is, but it's there all right."

"Shall we canter?" Anne asked. Her cousin agreed, and the conversation was dropped.

*

Two weeks after this meeting in the park, Daniel Dereham had a visit from Lord Neviss. They met once again in Daniel's suite at the Pulteney.

"I had an interesting conversation with Lord Grex a few days ago," Lord Neviss began, as Daniel took a sip of his brandy.

"Lord Grex? That's an odd name for an English lord."

"The Grex family is one of the oldest in the country," Lord Neviss explained. "There have been Grexes at Grex from the time records began to be kept. The present Earl of Grex, however, has not been a good steward of his family's history. He is deeply in debt, as is his son and heir."

Not a muscle moved in Daniel's face as he listened politely to this recital. Lord Neviss placed his brandy glass on the Queen Anne table in front of him and continued. "This is the situation as was told to me: the estate is entailed, but Lord Grex promised his son the money to pay his debts if Percival would legally relinquish his right of inheritance. That is the only way an entail can be broken, if the heir, who must be of age, signs papers relinquishing his right to the entailed property. Grex's son signed such papers. Unfortunately Lord Grex, who had expected to win the promised money on a race that was a 'sure thing,' lost the race and so didn't have the money. To pay his son, he took his daughter's dowry. Then, a few weeks ago, both the earl and his son once again lost large sums of money at Newmarket."

Lord Neviss looked at Daniel's impassive face and sighed. "So— to sum up this pitiful story—the Earl of Grex is willing to sell you his home with all its attending property. Also, as part of the bargain, he wishes you to marry his daughter, Lady Anne Grex."

"I wish everyone I did business with was as efficient as you," Daniel said with admiration. "An historic house, property, and an aristocratic wife all in one package. I'm impressed."

Lord Neviss grinned. "Do you think I have a future doing this sort of thing?"

Daniel laughed. "You might want to think about it. How did you find Lord Grex?"

Lord Neviss picked up his brandy and took another swallow. Still holding it in his hand, he said, "Everyone knows Grex is done up. He owes the banks, he owes the money-lenders, he's sold everything of value he owns. And his son is just as heavy a gambler, and just as poor a judge of horseflesh. In short, he's desperate. I asked him what he would need to pay off his debts."

"And?"

Lord Neviss named a sum and Daniel slowly shook his head. "I didn't think anyone could be that bad a judge of horseflesh."

Lord Neviss finished his brandy and replaced the glass on the table. "What do you think? Are you interested?"

"Yes, I'm interested. But I would like to see the place before I make an offer."

"What kind of offer are you thinking about?"

"I'll certainly cover his debts. What else I might add will depend upon what I see when I view the place."

"Fair enough. I imagine you want to meet with Lord Grex personally?"

"Yes."

"Lord Neviss stood up. "I'll go and see him and let you know what he says."

Daniel, who had risen with his guest, held out his hand. "I am very grateful to you, Lord Neviss, for your assistance in this matter. Is there any way I can show my gratitude other than by my thanks?"

Lord Neviss took the slender hand held out to him. "Friendship can't be bought with money, my friend. It's given freely. And I'm enjoying myself."

Daniel smiled. His smile was rare, and when it came it was beguiling. Lord Neviss smiled back and walked to the door. Before he departed, he turned and asked one more question, "What about the girl? Do you want to marry her?"

"I'll have to see her too," Daniel replied, and this time both men laughed.

CHAPTER FIVE

It was a rainy afternoon and Anne was in her bedroom with Miss Bonteen, who was straightening out the clothes in her charge's wardrobe. Anne, who had been standing by the window looking out at the rain, turned to her companion and said fretfully, "I don't like London any more, Bonny. I'm tired of the parties. I'm tired of saying the same things over and over again. I'm tired of the noise and the dirt and the bad air. And most of all, I'm tired of these young men who like me but don't think I'm good enough to marry."

"That's not true," Miss Bonteen protested. Mr. Martin Abbey is in love with you. You must see that."

"Perhaps he is, but his parents don't want him to marry me, and I certainly don't like the idea of being the unwanted daughter-in-law for the rest of my life."

Miss Bonteen sighed. "My love, what choice do you have? What choice has your father left you?"

"None," Anne replied bitterly. "He has stolen the money my mother left me, and thrown me upon the mercy of these hopeless suitors. Has anyone even mentioned to them that Papa said Grex could be my dowry?"

"I am sure Lady Moresack has told them, or has told their mamas. Unfortunately, my darling, Grex is more of a drawback than an asset. In its present state it's not fit to be a gentleman's residence."

Tears shone in Anne's eyes. She loved Grex, and the thought of it being abandoned hurt her unbearably.

"One of these young men will come up to scratch, Anne. I'm sure of it."

"Yes, but the thing is, Bonny, I don't want them to! I'm sick of them! I'm sick of being on parade, hoping someone will pick me." She threw herself into the upholstered chair in front of the fireplace. "Do you know what I'd like to do?"

Miss Bonteen closed the wardrobe door and turned to face Anne. "What would you like to do, dearest?"

"I'd like to get enough money to buy Grex from Papa. If I could own the house and the lake and the paddocks, and had enough income to keep one servant and one groom, I should be so happy!"

Miss Bonteen came over to Anne and rested a hand on her shoulder. "Don't torture yourself like this, my dear. You must do what women have done since Eve—you must find a man."

Anne bent her head. "I don't like Papa either," she said in a muffled voice. "And I don't like Percival. They are careless, selfish men, and I mean nothing to them. I'm a burden to be got rid of, that's all. They neither of them care a farthing for my happiness."

Miss Bonteen, who knew this was true, could find nothing reassuring to say to this girl whom she loved as a daughter.

*

Lord Grex was in alt when Lord Neviss told him about a possible buyer for Grex. Neviss reported back to Daniel that Grex would entertain an offer, and plans were made for the two men to travel to Yorkshire to view the house and property. So it was that, three days after Neviss' report, Daniel and Lord Grex were traveling to Yorkshire in a rented coach.

Daniel had been gratified to learn that Grex's property was situated in Western Yorkshire. Western Yorkshire was close by the Lancashire border, and Lancashire was the center of the English cotton and iron industries. Daniel's factory, which was northwest of the city of Manchester, should be easily reachable from western Yorkshire.

As the two men made the long drive to Yorkshire, Grex kept up a steady stream of eloquence about the many virtues of his home. Daniel wanted an historic home? Grex had been built in the days of Edward III! It was very historic. But it had also been kept up to date. Lord Grex assured Daniel he would be purchasing a house that boasted all of the features so dear to the hearts of English architects: oriel windows! twisted chimneys! long galleries! an inner courtyard with a fountain! Grex also had terraces and sundials and fishponds! It was exactly the sort of house Daniel was looking for—Lord Grex would guarantee that.

Daniel asked about the stables and the number of horses living there. Lord Grex was vague about the number of horses, but he assured Daniel that the stable was in use. When Daniel asked about the attached farms, Lord Grex said sadly that most of the farms had been abandoned because the men could make more money in the factories of Manchester than they could out of farming. However, Lord Grex continued, the home farm was still in operation. He had rented it to a fellow who worked it.

"I have an arrangement with Harding," his lordship explained to Daniel. "In return for use of the farm, he and his wife live in the house and take care of it. So there is always someone on the premises, and when my daughter and her companion were living at home, Mrs. Harding would clean their rooms and cook for them."

"There are no other servants?" Daniel inquired.

"I never go to Grex anymore, so there's no need to keep a household of servants with nothing to do."

"I see." What Daniel was seeing was more and more of the atrocious neglect the property had been subjected to during Lord Grex's tenure.

They arrived at Grex at four in the afternoon, as the sun was spilling a soft gentle light on the house and its windows. Daniel stopped the coach so he could get out and walk. As he stood on the drive, gazing at the mellow bricks of the old house, he felt a chill run up and down his spine. There it stood, his dream, there for the taking.

He tore his gaze away from the house and looked at the surrounding landscape. Unlike most great country homes, Grex did not stand in a park. Instead, low stonewalls divided the land into paddocks. In one of the far paddocks two horses and a pony stood next to each other, tails swishing as they watched the activity on the drive.

Grex had got out of the coach as well, and now Daniel turned to him. "Whose horses are they?" he asked.

"My daughter's mare and pony, and a gelding my son used to ride."

Daniel looked at all the empty paddocks and pictured them filled with gorgeous Arabian horses. He'd rather have a view of horses than a park he decided, as he followed Lord Grex into the house.

Mrs. Harding was at the door to greet them. "My lord." She greeted Grex with a small curtsey. "I received your letter and your room and a room for your guest are prepared."

"Thank you, Mrs. Harding. Will you have Harding carry the bags upstairs for us?"

"Of course, my lord. He was doing something in the garden, but he'll have heard the carriage coming down the drive. He'll be with us in a moment."

"Would you like me to show you around or would you like to rest first?" Lord Grex asked Daniel.

Daniel, who had never in his life rested in the afternoon, replied promptly, "I'd like to see the house."

His host took him from room to room, expounding upon all the important people who had slept here or played billiards there. But nothing Lord Grex could say was able to hide the devastating neglect the old house presented. The draperies had holes, the windows hadn't been washed within Daniel's lifetime, nor had the walls seen a paintbrush. There were empty places on the walls where he could see paintings had once hung. The rugs were threadbare, and all the furnishings were soiled and sagging. The ceilings looked extremely precarious. And dust had accumulated everywhere.

When the tour was finished Daniel began to add up in his head the amount of money it would cost to restore Grex to its former glory. As he stood with Lord Grex in the dining room, looking at the naked walls and bare china closet and sagging ceiling, the numbers ran higher and higher. And Daniel was certain the outbuildings would be in as bad, if not worse, condition. He shuddered to think of the stable. No horse of his would live there until everything was up to his standard.

It would take a fortune to make this estate the landmark he wanted it to be. But Daniel had a fortune, and he expected to earn another one from his factory. And he wanted Grex. The realization came to him, as he looked up at the filthy glass chandelier that hung in the dark, unlit hall. He wanted this home. His children would be born here, and they would never know the pain of rejection. He would send them to the best schools and they would marry into the best families. And his father would know that, on his own, he had surpassed the heritage his father had never granted him.

*

A week after the papers were signed and Grex had legally passed into the hands of Daniel Dereham, Lord Grex paid a visit to his daughter and gave her the news. Anne listened in silence, and when he had finished, she said accusingly, "Grex was supposed to be my dowry, Papa. Has the sale given you enough money to return my original dowry to me?"

Lord Grex's mouth tightened. He had the money, but he needed it for himself. He hadn't been well lately, and he planned to retire to Brighton to recuperate. "No, Anne," he said. "I'm afraid I can't replace your dowry."

Anne had never expected that he would. She raised her chin and stared directly into his washed-out blue eyes. "What do you suggest I do if I can't find a husband, Papa? I have no home to return to, and I can't remain here with Aunt Julia forever. Have you thought of me at all? Am I to beg for my bread on the street?"

"I have not forgot you Anne," the earl said with dignity, "and you won't have to beg on the street. I have found you a husband. The man who bought Grex has agreed to marry you."

This was a slight exaggeration on Lord Grex's part. Daniel had agreed to meet Anne and then decide whether or not he wished to marry her. But Lord Grex was not worried. Anne was a lovely girl, and she came from the oldest family in the country. Under other circumstances, Dereham wouldn't have been allowed near her. But circumstances change, Lord Grex told himself. And Anne would be able to remain at Grex, which he knew she loved.

"Are you going to tell me who this man is?" Anne asked. There was a white line down the middle of her slightly upturned nose. She was furious.

"It's Daniel Dereham," Lord Grex answered, his voice sounding slightly defensive. "You may have heard of him."

"Daniel Dereham!" Anne's cheeks flushed a rosy pink as she thought of the mystery man she had seen at a ball and on a horse trail. "Why on earth would someone like that want Grex?"

"I didn't ask him, my dear," her father said. "If you're so curious about his purpose you can ask him yourself. He is coming here this afternoon to have tea with you."

"Tea? With me? Will Aunt Julia be there?"

"No, Anne. It will be just you and Dereham. With Julia out of the way, you'll have a chance to charm him."

"What are you talking about, Papa? Have you told Aunt Julia about this scheme? She won't allow me to be alone in a room with a man she knows nothing about! We don't know who he is, or who his family are…" Her voice trailed off as her father stood and stared down at her, a set expression on his face.

"You have few choices, my girl. Julia tells me that none of your supposed suitors has come up to scratch, and she's afraid you might be left on the shelf. There's no future for you as a spinster. You have no sister or brother to take you into their household out of pity. The only home you have now belongs to someone else. If you really don't want to find yourself begging for your bread in the street, you'll do everything in your power to please this man."

He turned away from her and went to the door. "Think upon that, daughter, while you wait to meet Daniel Dereham. Be nice to him and he'll marry you. You'll have Grex to live in. You'll have your own horses and dogs." He opened the door and stepped into the hall. Before he closed it, he cast a look over his shoulder to where she sat appalled on the sofa. "Don't be stupid, Anne. Be nice to the man so he'll marry you."

CHAPTER SIX

Anne's knees were trembling as she climbed the stairs to her room. She was vastly relieved to find it unoccupied. She needed time to collect herself before she spoke to anyone, even Miss Bonteen, about what her father had just said to her.

Anne had never esteemed her father, but she never thought that he would betray her like this. He had taken the dowry her mother left her, and now he admitted to also taking her home, which he had said would replace the stolen dowry. She sat on the low chintz chair that faced the fireplace and shivered. It was late morning and there was no fire in her bedroom. She got up, pulled a shawl from the wardrobe, wrapped it around herself, and shivered some more.

What could she do? She searched every possibility her mind could imagine, but found no answer. She felt helpless and terrified, like an animal caught in a trap.

She tried to remember what she knew about Daniel Dereham. Jeremy had told her that he had gone to India and returned with a fortune. But where had he come from originally? Who were his people? What would he expect of his wife?

She thought back to their two encounters in Hyde Park. He had seemed nice. He had picked the stone out of Sedgwick's foot, and he had apologized for spooking Oliver. He had seemed nice. He owned a beautiful horse and he was a beautiful rider. He had seemed nice. Then she remembered Martin's comment about Dereham, that he owned a factory.

A factory. Anne's nostrils quivered as if they had caught the scent of something rotten. Men of Anne's class did not own factories. They owned land, which they had inherited from their ancestors, and they got their livelihood from that land by renting it out to tenants. The more land a man owned, the higher his rent roll, the wealthier he was. Grex had once had land like that, passed from generation to generation down the centuries. Then her grandfather and father had gambled it all away. The tenants, the land, the income—all gone because of two selfish and stupid men.

I hate him, Anne thought. I know it's a terrible sin to hate one's father, but I really hate him.

At that she broke down and had a good cry. When finally, her tears dried up, she poured water from the pitcher on her washstand and splashed it on her face. Then she went to the window and threw it open. She looked around the square, one of the most desirable places to live in all of London, and she thought about how much she wished she were back at Grex, the home of her blood. She wanted to go back to clean air and people she knew. She turned her back on some of the most expensive real estate in London, and thought that if she had to marry Daniel Dereham to get Grex, then, by damn, she would marry him.

*

Daniel too was taking a business-like approach to this prospective marriage. He had left boyhood behind when he took ship to India, and he had no romantic expectations as he stood at the door of the Moresacks' house in Grosvenor Square and lifted the knocker.

The door opened and a tall, grave butler appeared.

Daniel gave his name and added, "I am here to see Lady Anne."

"Very good, Mr. Dereham." The butler took Daniel's hat. "If you will follow me, sir."

They went halfway down a hallway that ran from the front of the house to the back. The butler knocked at a door on the right, opened it and announced, "Mr. Dereham, my lady."

Daniel stepped inside and an older woman crossed the Persian rug to greet him. "Good afternoon, Mr. Dereham," she said, offering her hand.

He bowed over it, and returned it to her.

"I am Anne's aunt...well, cousin, actually..." She laughed nervously. Daniel continued to look at her. "Lord Grex has desired me to leave you two young people alone, so I am going to do that. But I shall leave the door a little ajar, Mr. Dereham, and I will be nearby."

Daniel smiled with real amusement. "I have no intention of raping your niece, Lady Moresack. I left all my raping and pillaging behind when I left India."

Her hand went to her mouth and her blue eyes popped. She turned and looked at the girl who was seated behind the tea service. Anne said, "I promise I'll scream if he tries anything, Aunt Julia." The amusement in her voice matched his own.

"Yes, well..."

Daniel stood just inside the room and waited until Lady Moresack stepped into the hallway. Then he closed the door firmly and turned to Lady Anne.

She was very slender, with dark hair and dark eyes. He crossed the rug and, as he reached the table, he recognized her. "You're the girl from the park!"

She smiled. "Yes, I am. How is that beautiful Arabian of yours?"

"He's miserable. Hates being stuck in a London stable."

"Please, won't you sit?" She gestured and he sat.

She said, "I don't blame him. I'm pretty miserable in London myself."

That surprised him, and he looked at her more closely. Her eyes were a clear brown, the dark lashes very long. Her nose was small and slightly tilted upward, her lips finely modeled, her fair skin tinted pink on ivory. She was quite lovely, which was a relief. He had not been prepared to marry Grex' daughter if she'd been an eyesore.

"You prefer the country then?" he asked.

"Yes, I do." She looked at the teapot as if she would begin to pour, then changed her mind. For a moment her white teeth bit into her lower lip, then she straightened her already straight back and said, "Look, there doesn't seem to be much point carrying on with this pretext of taking tea. We're here for one purpose, and we might as well discuss it. I'll put my cards on the table if you'll put yours."

He was surprised and pleased. "I agree," he said pleasantly. "Why don't you begin? Are you willing to marry me and, if so, why?"

She shut her eyes, inhaled, opened them, clasped her hands in her lap, and said evenly, "As you observed, I am a country girl. I grew up in the country and Grex is the place I love best in the world. It's my home." For a moment her voice broke slightly. He watched in silence as she tightened the grip of her hands and steadied her voice. "I will marry you if I can live at Grex. I don't mind coming into London once in a while, but I want to spend most of my time at Grex." Her brown eyes looked directly and honestly into his. "That is why I am willing to marry you. I want my home back."

"Have you had other offers?" he asked curiously.

Her fine cheekbones grew pinker. "No," she said baldly.

"I find that difficult to believe. You have a famous family name and you are a beautiful woman."

A flicker of surprise showed in her eyes, then it was gone. "Thank you. I have no offers because I have no money, Mr. Dereham. Nor does my father present as the most desirable of in-laws. If you do choose to marry me I have nothing to bring you. My father took my dowry to pay off his debts. At that time he told me Grex would be my dowry, but then he sold it to you." Her gaze was straight as a lance. "I have nothing at all to bring you," she repeated.

He was impressed by her bravery. "Except a love of Grex," he said.

A faint smile answered his comment. "Yes. Except a love of Grex."

A little silence fell between them, then he spoke. "You have been honest with me and now I will be honest with you. Grex isn't much of a dowry, Lady Anne. In fact, it's more of a burden than anything else. It will take a very large sum of money to bring it back to what it once must have been, and few men will be able or willing to make such an investment. I am willing, however. I want to live in a

46

beautiful, gracious home, a home such as Grex will be when I finish renovating it. I would also like to create a small stud at Grex to breed pure Arabian horses. And I desire a wife who will be a gracious hostess for me, and a loving mother to my children. Are you willing to accept that role?"

"Yes," Anne said, "I am. And in me you will find a wife who knows everything there is to know about Grex and its property. I know the few tenants we have left and I know everyone who lives in the neighborhood. I can assure you that my husband will always be accepted by my friends."

He smiled at Anne, the devastating smile whose impact he perfectly understood. He was pleased with this young woman. She was trying to be calm and businesslike, but he saw through the façade to her essential innocence. As she herself had admitted, she was a young girl who loved her home. She probably had dogs and a favorite horse. It shouldn't be too hard to make her fall in love with him.

She was looking a little dazzled by the smile, and he held out his hand, "Shall we call it a deal, then?"

"I am willing," she said.

He kissed her hand and stood up. "Do you want me to get your aunt?"

"I supposed you'd better before she returns with a cadre of footmen to rescue me from your unwanted advances."

Daniel's laugh was genuine, and he started toward the door.

CHAPTER SEVEN

When Anne told Miss Bonteen that she had accepted Daniel Dereham's offer, her companion smiled with approval. "I didn't wish to influence your decision, dearest, but it is far better to be married than to be a spinster. I would not wish my situation on you for all the money in the world."

Anne was stunned. She had never thought Bonny felt such a dislike of her position, and she said as much.

"I am not unhappy!" Miss Bonteen hastened to reassure her. "I did not mean for you to take my words that way. I have been very fortunate, Anne. Because of your dear mother's early death, I have had a long-standing position with you. Governesses are commonly dismissed when their charges reach a certain age, which makes it necessary for one to find a new position. And when one is too old to be employed as a governess, one can only pray that some relative will step forward and give one a place to live out her days."

Anne had never thought about Miss Bonteen, or about governesses in general, in such a way. "It sounds like a grim life, Bonny," she said.

"It can be. And think, my dear, about yourself, and about what might have happened to you if Mr. Dereham had not made you this offer. Your father cannot afford to maintain you, and your brother...." She shrugged. Obviously, she felt the less said about Percival the better.

Anne was aghast. "Do you think I might have been forced to become a governess, Bonny?"

Miss Bonteen patted her hand. "I doubt it would have come to that, dearest. But what I am trying to say is this: For a woman to have a secure life, she needs a man to marry her."

Anne lifted her chin. "Mr. Dereham may be saving me from a life of poverty, but I am bringing him Grex. If he thinks he will find a poor, grateful and indebted wife in me, he will find himself much mistaken!"

49

"Of course he won't think that, Anne. He may have money, but without you he is only a wealthy interloper."

"That is true, Bonny," Anne said, and felt better.

*

Lady Moresack sent an announcement of the marriage to the *Morning Post*, setting off a flurry of gossip amongst the *ton*. The general consensus was that Lord Grex had done the only thing left open to him, and was fortunate to have landed such a wealthy husband for his daughter.

Lady Moresack was not pleased with the match. She felt that Anne should have waited. "If your father had not been so precipitous, Martin Abbey would have made you an offer," she said to Anne, as the two women took tea one afternoon. "He told me his father was softening."

"Please don't think you have failed me, Aunt Julia," Anne said. "I am not unhappy. This marriage means I can live the rest of my life at Grex, and that is what I want to do. And Mr. Dereham told me he plans to breed Arabian horses. I'm very excited about that."

"Horses are fine, but your uncle tells me Dereham has built a factory." Lady Moresack was close to weeping. "A cotton factory, Anne! You are marrying a man who owns a cotton factory!"

Anne had to suppress a smile. "It's very bad, I know. But none of my friends at home will cut me, Aunt Julia. The rector, the squire, the local gentry…. I can assure you they will all behave as the kind friends they have always been. They will accept Mr. Dereham for my sake."

Lady Moresack waved her hand in dismissal. "Of course the squire and the rector will receive the husband of Lady Anne Grex! But what of the other great houses in your neighborhood?"

"Mr. Dereham has been accepted by a number of London hostesses, Aunt Julia. But even if he weren't—please understand that I don't care. All that matters to me is being able to live in my beloved home."

Lady Moresack heaved a long sigh, patted Anne's arm and told her she was a brave girl.

*

Daniel wanted to be married at Grex, but he had a few requirements. "Before we tie the knot I would like to make at least a small attempt at sprucing the place up," he said to Anne. "Perhaps we could paint some of the downstairs rooms. They're quite depressing you know."

The young couple were sitting on a brocade sofa facing Lady Moresack, who occupied a tall wing chair close by. They had gathered to discuss the wedding. Anne, acutely conscious of her fiancé's closeness, was trying not to seem nervous. She said pleasantly, "What a good idea. Which rooms are you thinking of?"

"The rooms that still have intact ceilings," he answered in an equally pleasant tone. "I was petrified the ceilings in the dining room and library would come down on my head."

"Surely Grex can't be that bad," Lady Moresack protested.

"It is, Aunt Julia," Anne said sadly.

Daniel turned his crystalline gaze toward Lady Moresack. "The entire roof and most of the ceilings need to be replaced, as does most of the furniture. And the walls are bare. The paintings that must have hung there once are gone."

"Papa sold anything of value," Anne told her aunt. "We still have some pretty paintings, but, unfortunately, they aren't worth much."

Daniel looked at the painting that hung over Lady Moresack's chimney piece. "Is that one of your ancestors, my lady?" he asked.

"My husband's great grandfather," she replied loftily. "He was the first earl."

He nodded, his eyes still on the picture.

Lady Moresack said, "What servants do you still have, Anne, dear? Besides Miss Bonteen, that is."

"Bonny is not a servant!" Anne replied, her eyes flashing with indignation. "She is a part of my family."

Lady Moresack declined to pursue the matter of Miss Bonteen's position. "I merely wished to know how many people you employ, Anne. I rather think you will have to hire more."

"We just have the Hardings," Anne said in a low voice. "Papa lets him work the home farm and, in exchange for what he makes on the farm, Mr. and Mrs. Harding live in the house. She cooks for me and Bonny, and he fixes things when he has to."

Appalled silence from Lady Moresack.

Daniel, who had grown up with a mother, a stepfather and no servants, was less perturbed. "If we're going to have the wedding at Grex, then you had better hire some more servants," he said to Anne. "I'll open an account for you at my bank and you can draw on it as you need."

"Thank you," she murmured.

Her head was bent and the tender nape of her neck looked pink. Daniel realized his intended was embarrassed. "Don't worry," he said lightly. "The renovation of Grex is going to be a long project. Once this wedding is behind us, we'll have a better idea of where we stand."

She gave him a grateful smile. She really was very young, he thought, and wondered if he was asking too much of her. "Are you all right with this? Hiring people and fixing up the house before the wedding?"

Her chin lifted and the gaze that met his was steady. "Of course I am."

He believed her.

"May I ask where you intend to be while Anne takes care of things at Grex?" Lady Moresack's voice was dangerously calm.

"I have business in Ireland," Daniel returned. "I'm thinking of buying some land over there and I need to take a look at it."

Lady Moresack's eyes bulged and veins stood out on her neck. He heard Anne stifle a giggle. Her aunt said in dire tones, "You're going to Ireland?"

"It's not the ends of the earth, Lady Moresack," he said reasonably. "Why don't we set the wedding date for—oh six weeks from now? That will give Lady Anne time to get the house in order and I will be able to transact my business."

"That's fine with me, Aunt Julia," Anne said quickly. She looked worried that her aunt might have an apoplexy if she didn't take a breath. She turned to Daniel. "Just give me a list of the colors you like and don't like."

"I don't like gold," he said. "Or red. I like lighter colors—yellow, blue, green. I like a room to look as if it's filled with light."

"I'll have all the windows washed," Anne said. "You'll be surprised at the difference it makes."

He looked at Lady Moresack's frozen face and decided it might be a good idea to charm her a bit. He bestowed his most beguiling smile upon her and fifteen minutes later, as he was leaving, he heard that lady say to Anne, "Well. Mr. Dereham might not be the kind of man I wanted you to marry, but he can be remarkably agreeable when he chooses."

Daniel closed the door behind him and let the hovering footman show him to the door.

*

Anne and Lady Moresack remained behind to discuss the wedding in more detail. "Thank goodness Mr. Dereham did not insist on a London wedding," Lady Moresack said. "I was afraid he might wish to parade his conquest before all of the ton." She shuddered. "Like that dreadful cit who married the Ashville girl."

"Where did they get married?" Anne asked curiously.

"It was in St. Margaret's and the Ashvilles invited everybody. The groom had earned a fortune in some sort of trade and was very pleased with himself. Poor Amelia looked like a martyr going to the lions."

"Did you go to the wedding Aunt Julia?"

"Of course," came the satisfied reply. "It was truly horrendous."

"Well then, Mr. Dereham showed sensitivity," Anne said, happy to find as many good points about her future husband as possible. "He really loved Grex, Aunt Julia. He wants to spend a ton of money to bring it back to what it should be."

Lady Moresack sighed. "That is a good sign, I suppose. And he certainly is a handsome man, Anne. At least he will be pleasant for you to look upon. One must hope that you won't have to look upon him very often, however. With his factory," a shudder accompanied this word, "and his property in Ireland, let's hope he won't be around to bother you too often. Give him a son and he should be happy to leave you alone."

Anne felt her cheeks grow hot. The marriage her aunt was describing sounded dreadful to her, but Aunt Julia was right. Daniel Dereham was hardly marrying her because he liked her, let alone loved her. He was marrying her for Grex, and she was marrying him for the same reason. They may turn out to have little in common, but at least they would be as one in regard to Grex. And that was what was important.

Wasn't it?

CHAPTER EIGHT

Anne wanted to wear an ordinary morning dress for her wedding, but Lady Moresack insisted on buying her a proper wedding gown. Nor did she accept Anne's plan to be married in the house with only her close family present.

"You must be married in the village church," Lady Moresack declared. "The townspeople and surrounding gentry will expect it. You don't want to give rise to any gossip about why you are marrying Mr. Dereham, Anne. You know how country people are. They will think the whole thing is havey-cavey and will speculate about you having to get married. That is definitely not the picture you want to present to the neighborhood. It will also be a good opportunity for people to see your bridegroom. One thing I will say for him, he makes a splendid appearance."

Anne talked the matter over with Miss Bonteen, who agreed with the countess. "You must be open about this marriage, dearest. You must look happy. You do not want to find yourself fodder for the gossips! They have enough to talk about already. Mr. Dereham is not the sort of man they would be expecting you to marry."

Anne was sensible enough to realize that when the two ladies who truly had her welfare in mind told her the same thing, she would be wise to listen. She gave in and went shopping with Lady Moresack. They chose a slender, high-waisted gown of white and silver, and added a long silk veil. The veil attached to the center of her hair, and fell down her back almost to the hem of her gown. It was very pretty and it made Anne begin to feel a little bit like a real bride.

Anne and Miss Bonteen left for Yorkshire the day after the dress had been fitted. Aunt Julia would deliver it when she came to Grex for the wedding.

For Anne the trip home seemed to last forever. She longed with all her heart to see Grex again, and when Lord Moresack's coach finally turned into the lane, and the rambling old brick building and its surrounding stone-enclosed paddocks, rose before her, she began to cry.

Miss Bonteen patted her shoulder. "There, there, dearest. It will be all right," she murmured.

"It's just...I'm so happy to be home!" Anne said, applying a delicate handkerchief to her wet cheeks. She sniffed and said, "Just think, Bonny, if Martin Abbey had proposed to me, I would never have come here again. I would have lived in a strange place—and with parents-in-law who didn't approve of me." She turned her head away from the window to look at Miss Bonteen. "Perhaps, instead of dreading this marriage I should be thinking, Thank God for Mr. Dereham."

Miss Bonteen patted her hand. "It could have been worse, my love. It certainly could have been worse."

*

The three weeks that followed Anne's arrival at Grex went by in a whirl. She was busy from dawn to dusk trying to make a few rooms livable before the wedding. Daniel had told her he would take care of the painters, and two days after her arrival twelve men duly showed up at Grex's back door, paintbrushes in hand. While eleven of them went to work preparing the rooms Anne had designated for painting, she sat with the supervisor and picked out colors. Then, while some of the men were painting and some were washing windows, Anne scoured the house for suitable furniture. Fortunately, her mother had gotten rid of a good deal of the heavy Jacobean furniture that used to clutter the house, and had bought lighter pieces by Chippendale, Sheraton, Hepplewhite and their ilk. Anne hired a few men from the village to polish up the tables, bookcases, cupboards, highboys and lowboys she collected until their wood glowed. She spread these between the first-floor parlor and the breakfast room. Most of the rugs weren't worth saving, so she had the men take them up and polish the wood floors. She also bought new linens for the earl's bedroom and ripped the ancient, dust-laden canopy off the bed. One of the highboys went in the dressing room for Daniel's clothes, and she brought her own chest in from her room.

She got a funny feeling in her stomach while she was working on the bedroom. It was hard to believe that in a few weeks she would be sharing this room, this bed, with Daniel Dereham. This was not a thought she cared to dwell on, and she banished it quickly whenever it rose to the surface of her mind.

*

Daniel arrived at Grex four days before the wedding. As he drove his curricle down the lane he could see the old house in the distance. The bright afternoon sunshine turned its rose-colored bricks to gold, and all of its many windows sparkled in the glowing light. He lowered his hands and stopped his horses so he could sit for a moment and look at it.

Grex. One of the oldest homes in all of England, and it was his. The feeling that welled up inside of him was indescribable—a feeling of possessiveness, of accomplishment, of triumph. He had done it. He had left behind the cottage where he had grown up. He had left behind the laborers and stable lads who had been his friends. He owned this house, and in three days he would marry an earl's daughter, a woman from his father's untouchable aristocracy. They—those inhabitants of that world he both wanted and hated at the same time—they might look down their noses at him now, but he knew his was the star of the future. Grex was the first step, and Lady Anne was the second. She was the real thing, an earl's daughter, born to be a lady. No one would dare to look down his nose at Lady Anne. And, most important of all, no one would dare to despise their children. They would carry his dream into the future. Everything he had ever wanted since he had worked his way to India at the age of sixteen was within his grasp. Daniel lifted his hand and his horses moved on, carrying him to his destiny.

*

As well as help for the house, Anne had hired men to work on fixing up the stable. She had also told Frankie, the elderly groom and the only one left to care for the horses, to hire a few stable lads to help him. She assumed Daniel would come by carriage, and it was unthinkable that there should be no one to care for his horses.

She was in the stable inspecting the work when Timmy, one of the new stable lads, came running to find her. "He's here, my lady, and he's driving two bang-up horses!"

Oh no, Anne thought in despair. She had planned to meet her fiancé in Grex's newly painted parlor. She had pictured herself wearing an elegant blue afternoon dress, showing him around the marvels she had wrought in such a short time. Now here she was in her oldest riding skirt, with her hair tied back in a pigtail and an ancient pair of boots on her feet.

Oh well, there was nothing to be done. Anne lifted her chin, affixed a welcoming expression to her face, and went to greet her future husband, her spaniel trotting at her heels.

Daniel was standing at his horses' heads talking to Frankie when she came out. As she watched, Frankie patted an arched chestnut neck and said something. Daniel laughed, then turned his head as he spotted her coming toward him. He gave her that beguiling smile she remembered so well, and she felt her heart begin to beat faster. Really, she thought, annoyed with herself, it should be against the law to be so handsome.

She smiled back and held out her hand as they met. Then, as she remembered she was wearing her old, stained work gloves, she tried to snatch it back. He captured it, however, and held it snugly with his own as he bowed over it politely.

"Sorry about the gloves," she said as he straightened up. "I knew you were coming, and I intended to change my clothes, but the time rather got away from me."

"That can often happen when one is engaged with horses," he said amiably. He looked down at Dorothy, who was wagging her tail ferociously. "And who is this little miss?" he asked.

Anne smiled. "This is Dorothy. We missed each other terribly when I was in England."

Daniel had bent down and was now scratching behind Dorothy's long ears. She looked blissful. When he stood up again she shook her head and began to sniff his boots. He said to Anne, "Come and meet my chestnuts. They're friendly."

"They're beautiful," she said sincerely as she walked beside him up to the horses. They were perfectly matched with identical white blazes down the front of their faces. Their manes were almost as fine as a lady's hair.

"This is Romeo," he said, patting the horse on the left, "and this one is Roger."

"Romeo?" Anne smiled as she patted the shining neck.

"Yes. He hasn't yet figured out he's a gelding. I keep him well away from the mares."

Anne laughed. "They're not Arabians, though."

"No. I could only bring a few horses home with me. Amit, the black stallion you saw with me in the park, is one of them. I also brought two mares. Those three will be the bedrock of my stud. I'm hoping I can find a few more mares here in England."

Roger nickered and Daniel changed sides to pat him as well. "I daren't show any more favor to one than the other. They keep account."

"Where do you keep Amit?" Anne asked.

"I'm renting a farm near my factory and he's there at the moment. I didn't want to bring him here until you have stalls to hold them."

"We've been working on them," Anne said. "We rebuilt six of the stalls and they're all strong enough to hold a stallion. Will Amit be all right in the same barn as my mare and pony?"

"Let's take a look at the stalls now," he suggested. "They'll probably be fine for Romeo and Roger, but I'm not certain I want to put Amit in the same barn as a mare."

To Anne's relief, Daniel was pleased with work that had been done on the stable. The carpenters had knocked down all of the old stalls and reinforced the stable's walls and windows before building the new stalls. Originally the stable had held twenty horses and a large part of it now stood empty.

"I'm surprised you could get so much done in so short a time," Daniel said, looking around the stable, which smelled pleasantly of hay and straw.

"I had the stable work started before the work on the house," Anne said. "I thought the horses were more important."

Daniel gave her an approving smile. "Good girl," he said.

A little to her consternation, Anne found herself enormously pleased by the compliment. Why should Daniel Dereham's opinion mean so much to her? She hadn't done the work for him, she had done it for the horses.

She said coolly, "The stable we're standing in was always used for riding horses. I'm told that in the days of my great-grandfather it housed hunters, hacks, ladies' riding horses and ponies for the children. The other two stables housed the carriage horses and farm horses." She sighed. "We haven't had our own carriage horses in years, and the farms have been reduced to just the one that Mr. Harding works."

She began to walk out of the stable and he followed. "What do you think? Would it be safe to stable Amit here?" she asked when they were back standing in the sunlight.

"I'd like to build an even larger stall for him, away from the mares. Perhaps we could put the carriage horses in between so he doesn't get a whiff of them."

"Would you like to look at the other stables to see if they might be useful?"

He shook his head. "I had a look at them when I was here with your father. I think it would be easier to just tear them down and build something new."

Anne thought of the holes in the roof, of the rotted planks that used to be stalls and felt her face flush with embarrassment. "I'm afraid that neither my father nor my grandfather was a good steward of this property," she said in a low voice. "Grex was a beautiful home once, but they let it decay, and now…" Her voice trailed away.

He looked at her with slightly narrowed eyes. He wasn't a big man, he was of average height and slimly built. But when one was with him one felt a kind of power. It was a distinctly male power, and part of Anne responded to it. The other part of her was afraid. What was it going to be like to be married to Daniel Dereham?

Then he smiled, that beguiling smile that was so attractive. "You love Grex, don't you, Anne?"

It was the first time he had called her by her name. "Yes," she said. "It's my home, and I'm very glad to be back here." She inhaled deeply, then made herself say, "I'm glad you asked me to marry you."

His eyebrows, black as coal above those light blue eyes, lifted. Then he said, "We'll make Grex a beautiful home once again, I promise you. It's the kind of place I've always wanted. It gives off a feeling of being…rooted."

He had said it perfectly. "Yes," she said with approval. "That's it. It's been here for centuries and centuries of time, and it is rooted."

He looked around the paddocks, then asked, "Are those your horses in the far paddock?"

"Yes. The mare is Molly. She was bred to race but she wasn't fast enough. I've had her since she was four and she's seventeen now. The chestnut pony with her is Tucker, my very first horse. He's twenty-seven."

"You must take good care of your horses," he said. "A twenty-seven-year-old pony, and a seventeen-year-old thoroughbred…." He nodded in approval.

Anne was pleased by the compliment. "They've always been healthy, thank goodness. Molly has the sweetest disposition, and Tucker," she laughed, "well, he's a pony. Molly adores him and he tolerates her."

"Hmm." He was watching Molly as she grazed contentedly. She was a bay and her dark brown coat shone in the afternoon sun.

"I met your horses; would you like to meet mine?" Anne asked.

"Yes," he said. "I would."

He gestured for her to precede him, and together they walked along the dirt path that separated the paddocks, Dorothy running in front of them. "The grass looks as if it would be nice and nutritious," he said as they went by one paddock after another.

"We have wonderful grass here." Anne was beginning to feel comfortable with this young man. He asked all the right questions, he hadn't made any sarcastic remarks about the state of the stables, and he wanted to meet Molly.

They stopped at the gate that led into the paddock and Molly whinnied and came trotting over. The pony wasn't far behind her. Anne reached into her pocket and pulled out a bit of carrot for them both.

"She certainly doesn't look seventeen," Daniel said with admiration. "We'll have to keep Amit away from her. She's just the type of mare he fancies."

"We'll put Romeo and Roger in between them in the stable," Anne promised.

They turned away from the paddock and began to walk back toward the house. He said, "Do you think I might get something to eat and drink?"

Anne was mortified. "Of course! I'm so sorry! How stupid of me to keep nattering on about horses when you…"

"You weren't nattering," he interrupted. "I asked to see your mare, but now I'm ready for some refreshment."

"So am I," Anne said. "I hope you'll like the new paint. Some of it is still damp."

"I'm sure I'll like it—as long as it isn't gold?"

"It's not gold," she assured him. "The colors are blue and cream."

"Good," he said.

He's being very nice, Anne thought as she preceded him into the house. I hope he stays this way.

CHAPTER NINE

Anne's wedding day dawned with high blue skies and fluffy white clouds. She felt preternaturally calm as Miss Bonteen helped her dress in her beautiful silver and white wedding gown. The house had been full the last two days, and Anne had been kept busy. Between consulting with the new cook, with Mr. Corby, the minister who was to marry her, and with Aunt Julia, she had little time to herself. Which she thought might be a good thing—it left her too tired to worry when she went to bed at night.

Joining the group visiting Grex was Miss Alice Francis—an elderly cousin of Aunt Julia's whom she had brought along for no reason Anne could see, Anne's fiancé, and Mr. Denver, the man who was to be Daniel's groomsman at the wedding.

None of Anne's family knew what to make of Mr. Denver. He was a well-spoken man, a good-looking man, and his manners were perfectly correct. But there was something not quite right about him; he was not "one of us." Anne had seen Aunt Julia monitoring him at table, and if Aunt Julia hadn't found anything to complain about, then there wasn't anything. He was tall, taller than Daniel, and he had wide shoulders, brown hair and hazel eyes. Daniel had introduced him as an old friend from India days, and that was all they knew. Aunt Julia was put out about the whole thing.

"Just who is this Denver person?" she had complained to Anne when Mr. Denver first arrived. "Where does he come from? Who are his people? Surely you have asked Mr. Dereham to explain him, Anne!"

Anne, Aunt Julia, Miss Francis and Miss Bonteen were all seated in the newly painted drawing room drinking tea. Anne put down her cup and sighed. "Aunt Julia, it isn't easy to ask Daniel questions about personal matters."

"I think you have the right to know about a man who is to be in your wedding party," Aunt Julia said. She picked up a biscuit and vigorously broke it in half. "That young man must be made to understand that he's no longer a vagabond from God knows where.

He's the master of Grex! He's somebody! He can't have nobodies standing up for him at his wedding."

Anne said patiently, "Aunt Julia, I can see nothing at all wrong with Mr. Denver. He is pleasant, well informed, and a friend of Daniel's. Surely Daniel should be allowed to pick the person he wishes to stand up for him at his own wedding."

Miss Francis said in her thin quivering voice, "I believe Mr. Denver has a tattoo on his wrist, Lady Anne. I saw it when his sleeve pulled up a little last night at dinner."

"You didn't tell me that, Alice!" Lady Moresack said.

"The opportunity never came up, Julia," that lady replied with composure.

Anne tried not to roll her eyes. In the scheme of things, she thought, Mr. Denver was the very least of her problems.

She had indeed tried to bring up the subject of Mr. Denver with Daniel, and had come up against the proverbial brick wall. In the pleasantest way possible, he had made it known that Mr. Denver was none of her business. Privately, she had agreed with him. So now she folded her hands in her lap and said cajolingly, "I know you're upset about this marriage, Aunt Julia. I know you're worried about me. I know you wanted me to marry Martin Abbey. But I am happy with the match. I am living in the home I love, and Daniel has been a very pleasant companion these last few days. Please don't worry. I shall be fine."

Lady Moresack sniffed and touched a handkerchief to her eyes. "I am very fond of you, Anne. You know that. I am only thinking of your happiness."

"I know you are, Aunt Julia," Anne said. "But I am happy. Daniel is willing to spend a great deal of money to restore Grex, and he wants me to take charge of the renovation." She gave Lady Moresack her lovely warm smile. "Don't worry about me, Aunt. When Grex is looking better, I'll invite you for a visit, and you will see for yourself how happy I am."

Lady Moresack sniffed again, put her handkerchief away and said, "You are such a brave girl, Anne. If anyone can be happy in this situation, it is you."

*

As she stood in the back of the church with Miss Bonteen, Anne thought of her aunt's remark. She had been feeling perfectly fine until she reached the church steps, then her stomach and chest had tightened, and her heart had begun to thump. She shut her eyes and prayed hard that she wouldn't faint.

"The church is filled," Miss Bonteen remarked complacently. "Everyone in the village and local countryside has come."

Anne let her eyes drift over the filled pews. As Miss Bonteen had pointed out, most of the people she had seen in church every Sunday of her life—the local gentry, the village shopkeepers and tradesmen—were there. She looked down the aisle and saw Mr. Corby, the vicar who had baptized her. He was in full ecclesiastical regalia. Standing in front of him their backs to her, were her soon-to-be husband and his groomsman, both immaculately dressed in formal black tailcoats. Her father and brother were seated in the first pew, which had belonged to the Grex family since one of her ancestors had built the church several centuries earlier. Aunt Julia was with them, with her cousin Miss Francis.

That's my entire family, Anne thought. Papa, Percival and Aunt Julia. Except now there would be Daniel.

Miss Bonteen patted her arm. "Are you ready, dearest? The music should begin momentarily."

Anne turned to look at her old governess with tears in her eyes. "I love you, Bonny," she said. "You're the only real family I've ever had."

Tears sprung in Miss Bonteen's eyes as well. "I will never desert you, my love. Always remember that."

Anne swallowed, and the organ began to play. Miss Bonteen nodded encouragingly. Anne gripped the fragrant bouquet she was holding and began to walk slowly down the aisle. Miss Bonteen, clad in a simple blue gown with a figured bodice, followed behind. The congregation rose and turned to get their first look at the bride.

I'm making a terrible mistake, Anne thought as she walked past the smiles of everyone she knew. I don't know this man at all, and here I am going to pledge my life to him.

She cast a quick glance at Daniel as she came closer to the altar. What was she doing with a man who looked like that? How could she expect him to be loyal to her? He knew as little about her as she knew about him. He didn't care a fig for her, he was marrying her to get Grex. She knew that, had been fine with it, but now…when it was too late…

She had reached the altar and Daniel moved to stand beside her. She glued her eyes on Reverend Corby, but every cell of her body was aware of the man beside her, of that strange power he seemed to exude, even when he was just standing quietly, as he was now.

Mr. Corby began, "Dearly Beloved, we are gathered together here in the sight of God, and in the face of this congregation, to join together this man and this woman in holy matrimony; which is an honorable estate, instituted of God in the time of man's innocency, signifying unto us the mystical union that is betwixt Christ and his Church…"

It was too hot in here. Anne's vision blurred. She blinked, squeezed her hands around the stem of her bouquet, and commanded herself not to faint.

A warm hand covered her grip on the bouquet. Startled she looked at Daniel. He squeezed her rigid hands gently, shot her a quick smile, then turned back to the vicar.

"First it was ordained for the procreation of children…"

Children. Aunt Julia had talked to her last night about children and about how they were made. She had heard all about her duty and how she must bear sexual congress, unpleasant though it may be.

"…ordained for a remedy against sin, and to avoid fornication…"

Fornication. Anne knew what that word meant. Would Daniel humiliate her by fornicating with other women after they were married? Aunt Julia had spoken to her about that too: Heaven knows what he got up to while he was in India. One can only hope he has the decency to be discreet. But your duty, my dear, is to ignore it. Whatever he might do with other women, ignore it. Cultivate your own friends and your own diversions. That is the way a lady behaves.

The vicar had reached the vows. Miss Bonteen gently turned Anne toward Daniel, who had already turned to her. She listened as the Vicar said to Daniel: "Wilt thou have this woman to thy wedded wife, to live together after God's ordinance in the holy estate of matrimony? Wilt thou love her, comfort her, honor, and keep her in sickness and in health; and, forsaking all others, keep thee only unto her, so long as ye both shall live?"

Daniel's crystal blue eyes held hers. "I will," he said firmly.

The vicar turned to her: "Wilt thou have this man to thy wedded husband, to live together after God's ordinance in the holy estate of matrimony? Wilt thou obey him, and serve him, love, honor and keep him in sickness and in health; and, forsaking all others, keep thee only unto him, so long as ye both shall live?"

Daniel's eyes were smiling at her. Anne lifted her chin and said resolutely, "I will."

Next Anne's father upheld his brief role as the man who giveth this woman to be married to this man, and Daniel took her hand as he pledged his troth to her. He was so calm, so steady, and that helped her. She returned his pledge softly: "I Anne Elizabeth Sophia take thee Daniel Patrick to my wedded husband, to have and to hold from this day forward, for better for worse, for richer for poorer, in sickness and in health, to love, cherish, and to obey, till death us do part, according to God's holy ordinance; and thereto I give thee my troth."

Daniel placed a ring on the third finger of her left hand and said, "With this ring I thee wed, with my body I thee worship, and with all my worldly goods I thee endow."

At last Mr. Corby had come to the end, "For as much as Daniel Patrick and Anne Elizabeth Sophia have consented together in holy wedlock, and have witnessed the same before God and this company, and thereto have given and pledged their troth each to other, and have declared the same by giving and receiving of a ring, and by joining of hands, I pronounce that they be man and wife together, in the name of the Father, and of the Son, and of the Holy Ghost. Amen."

As the vicar said the blessing over them, all Anne could think was, It's over. It's done. I am married to Daniel Patrick Dereham.

They walked down the aisle together and stood side by side, along with her father and Percival, to receive the good wishes of the congregants. Everyone congratulated Daniel, and wished her well. The squire and his wife, the Bestons who lived in Ivy House, the Ralphs who lived in Saye House, the Bartons, the Housers, the Smythes, the Woodhouses, all of the local gentry were there in their best attire and would be coming back to the house for a wedding breakfast. Then there were the villagers, people whom Anne had done business with ever since she had taken over the reins of the household — the blacksmith (it had been a very long time since Grex could afford to keep its own blacksmith), the shoemaker, the carpenter, Mrs. Lewis who owned the local market, Mr. Holt who owned the feed store, Mr. Daily who was the apothecary...all the people who served the needs of the local farmers and townsfolk. They had their wives and children with them, and everyone was dressed in their best clothes.

They looked so happy for her, and Anne realized it had been right to have the wedding in the church. These good people deserved a celebration, and Daniel had rented a tent to be set up on the back lawn to serve food and drink to them, as they did not qualify as gentry and could not be invited into the house.

For a wedding trip Daniel was taking Anne to Heysham, a pretty village located on the shore of Morecambe Bay. He had never been there himself, but he had heard from "people who know" that there was a fine hotel with views of the Irish Sea, and several places of interest to explore. They were going for a week, to give time for all of the visitors to clear out of the house, Daniel had said when he told her of his plan.

Anne had been pleased. The idea of getting used to a husband while her family was still around was not an idea she had relished. But now, as she changed into her travel dress in her childhood bedroom, the thought of being alone with Daniel Dereham was making her nervous. Perhaps staying at Grex, with other people around, would have been a better idea she thought, as she nervously took her place in the carriage Daniel had rented.

Before she went out to the carriage, she kissed Bonny, her father, her brother, her aunt and her cousin goodbye. "You must all come for a visit when we have finished our renovations," she had said, smiling as brilliantly as she could.

Everyone agreed, and came out of the house to wave goodbye. Her father helped her into the carriage, her husband stepped in from the other side, the doors closed and they were off. She was alone with Daniel Dereham, the stranger she had married.

CHAPTER TEN

The setting sun was hanging over the waters of Morecambe Bay when their carriage pulled up to the front of a large, elegant looking stone hotel located on the waterfront. Daniel helped Anne out of the carriage and took her arm as they went inside. All of Daniel's arrangements were in order, and a liveried servant escorted them up a flight of stairs to their home for the following week.

The suite of rooms was lovely, with painted white and gold furniture that looked French to Anne. There was a balcony off the sitting room that looked directly over the bay, and another with the same view in the single large, airy bedroom.

"I don't know about you, but I'm hungry," Daniel said as they stood on the sitting room balcony while more servants brought in their luggage. "I understand the food in the dining room is very good. Would you like some dinner?"

"Yes," Anne answered. Anything that postponed the inevitable ending to this day sounded appealing to her.

There were two dressing rooms off the single bedroom and a hotel maid came directly after Anne rang the bell. The maid helped her change her travel dress for a pale pink gown that had a deeply scooped neck. The soft silken material was gathered under her breasts a la empire, and it swirled around her legs as she went down the stairs with her husband to a dinner she didn't think she could possibly eat.

As the new bride and groom entered the dining room, a number of the couples already dining looked up to see who had come in. Anne kept her eyes on the waiter's back, but she could feel the looks, and they weren't directed at her. As the waiter pulled out the chair to seat her, she distinctly heard a female voice say in French, *"Qui est cet homme beau? Il a visage d'un ange de Michel-Ange!"*

Anne glanced at Daniel but his expression never changed. What thoughts were behind that finely sculpted face she wondered. He was so different from anyone she had ever known. What had motivated him to want a house like Grex so much that he had agreed to marry a penniless girl to get it? He was a mystery to her, a mystery who looked like an angel.

Once they were seated and looking at a menu that featured seafood, the waiter asked Daniel about wine. He ordered champagne. Anne never drank wine, but she held her tongue. They studied the menus in silence, and when the waiter came back with the champagne, Anne picked up her glass and took a sip. To her surprise, she liked it. She took another sip to confirm her first impression.

Daniel was watching her with a smile. She said, "I've tasted champagne before and didn't like it, but this is delicious."

"I'm glad you approve."

As course followed course, Daniel ate hungrily, but Anne only managed to choke down a small amount of food. She asked him about India, and listened with interest as he told her about the Maharajah he had worked for and how his state was run. Every time the waiter returned and saw her empty glass, he poured more champagne into it. Toward the end of the meal Daniel said, "I'm pleased you like the wine, but if you have much more of it you're going to have a bad headache in the morning."

But Anne liked the way the wine was making her feel, and she waved her hand dismissively at Daniel and asked him another question. She felt pleasantly distanced—from Daniel, from the hotel, from everything. When the waiter removed her plate and went to pour more wine into her glass, Daniel held up his hand. "You've had enough, I think. It's time we went upstairs."

Anne stared at him in bewilderment. "We haven't had pudding."

"You haven't even eaten your dinner, you don't want pudding."

He came around the table to offer her his arm. She stood, then frowned at the floor, which seemed to be moving rather like the waves in the bay. She rested her hand on the sleeve of his black coat, blinked twice, and said, "Oh dear."

"Exactly. Can you make it to the stairs or do I have to carry you?" He sounded amused.

She lifted her chin and the movement made her dizzier. "I can walk," she said loftily.

"Hold onto my arm."

Anne already had a death grip on his arm. She put one foot in front of the other as she walked with him through an oddly tilting world. She wasn't nervous any longer; the champagne had given her a glorious feeling of detachment.

The detachment lasted, even after Daniel left her in her dressing room with the waiting maid. She stood like an obedient child as the maid undressed her and slipped a thin ivory satin nightgown over her head. Anne looked down at the nightgown, which had been given to her by Aunt Julia, and said to the maid, "Isn't it pretty?"

"Very pretty, my lady. There now, your hair is all brushed out. You look very beautiful, if I may say so."

"I do?"

Anne walked over to the pier glass and looked into the mirror. She saw a tall, slim girl with porcelain perfect skin and long shining hair streaming down her back. Her eyes looked very large and dark. "I think I might have drunk too much champagne," she confided to the maid.

"Perhaps that's not such a bad thing, my lady. Now you should get yourself into bed. Mr. Dereham will be waiting for you."

"He's my husband," Anne said with dignity.

"Yes, my lady, I know. Let me open the door for you."

"I'm not afraid," Anne confided. "I'm very brave. My Aunt Julia always tells me how brave I am."

"I'm sure you are, my lady."

With that pleasantly disinterested feeling still intact, Anne pushed the door open and went into the bedroom. "He's not here," she frowned, and turned to the maid who was in the act of closing the dressing room door and departing. "Where is he?" Anne asked.

"He'll be along shortly, I'm sure." The maid came into the room, took Anne's arm and steered her to the bed. She lifted the satin coverlet and coaxed Anne to get in between the silk sheets, which Anne did with great dignity. "Just stay there," the maid said.

"I will," Anne promised. She was feeling sleepy but before she could close her eyes and get comfortable, the door to the second dressing room opened and Daniel came in. He was wearing a black brocade dressing gown and his feet were bare.

Anne frowned at him. "Where are your shoes?"

He said, "I don't need shoes, Anne. I'm going to bed. You don't have shoes on, do you?"

"No."

He sat on his side of the bed and regarded her with amusement. "I gather you don't drink wine very often."

"No. I don't like it, and it's too expensive." She looked at him. "I'm not afraid anymore," she informed him. "I'm very brave, and nothing you do to me will be worse than losing Grex."

"I'm glad to hear that," he replied, taking off his dressing gown and getting into bed beside her. "Do you know what we're going to do tonight?"

She stared at his bare torso. For so slim a man he had a lot of muscles. "Aunt Julia told me," she said. "And I've seen animals, of course. But don't worry. I won't cry. I'm very br…"

"I know, you're very brave."

"Yes," she said, lifting her chin and exposing the graceful line of her long elegant neck.

"Do you think you're brave enough to kiss me?"

He got a long appraising stare in return. Then she said haughtily. "Yes."

"Then come here to me," he said softly.

Anne, who was indeed very brave, went.

*

When she awoke the following morning, it was to find Daniel watching her, the sheet pushed back from his shoulders, his chin resting on his folded arms. "Good morning," he said in a soft voice.

Anne looked back into those crystalline blue eyes, remembered last night, and flushed.

He gave her a boyish grin. "There's nothing to be embarrassed about, Annie. We're married, remember."

Every inch of Anne's body remembered vividly.

"I hope I managed to disprove your Aunt Julia's notions about 'marital congress'."

He looked flushed and happy, with his hair sticking up like a little boy's and his celestial blue eyes smiling at her.

She relaxed and smiled back. "You certainly did."

There was faint stubble on his cheeks and chin, which for some reason made him seem even more attractive. His shoulders and abdomen looked very strong. He held out an arm and said, "Come and cuddle a bit."

Anne slid over and nestled her head into his shoulder. It fit as if it belonged there.

"What would you like to do today?" he asked.

"What are my choices?"

"We could walk on the beach, walk on the cliffs, rent horses and ride along the cliffs, rent a boat and view the cliffs from the bay..."

"I seem to see a pattern here," Anne said.

"The cliffs?"

"The cliffs."

"I gather they're one of the main attractions. The other is an 11th century church—St. Peter's—which is attached to the ruins of an equally old chapel that St. Patrick is said to have established. Those are the respectable visitors' sites. There is also another hotel famous for its gambling rooms."

Anne stiffened. "Do you like to gamble, Daniel?" she asked tensely.

He touched his lips to her hair and said, "I grew up poor, Annie, and now I have a fortune. I promise you, I have no plans to be poor again. No, I don't gamble."

"I'm glad," she said, relief washing through her body.

"You are never to worry about losing your home," he said sternly. "Grex is my home too now, and I give you my word I will never give it up."

She turned her face into his shoulder and said in a muffled voice, "Thank you, Daniel. Thank you."

He kissed her ear. "You're such a sweetheart, Annie," he said softly. "So pretty and so honest and so very sweet." He turned her face up to his and lowered his mouth to hers. A moment later she responded by reaching up to lock her hands around his neck. His mouth moved from her mouth to her neck to her breasts, and she shuddered with anticipation. Aunt Julia hadn't known what she was talking about.

CHAPTER ELEVEN

Anne was in love. Overnight her whole idea of herself had changed. Her body, her heart, her brain, nothing was the same. She felt the light material of her dress as it swished against her legs when she walked. She felt her mother's lightweight gold necklace touching the skin of her tender breasts. Brushing her hair, she felt Daniel's hands as he ran them slowly through the silky mass. When he took her arm to go into dinner, she felt his touch in her stomach.

They spent the entire morning of the second day of their wedding trip in bed, and in the afternoon, they explored the two churches. The following days they also remained in bed for the morning, but in the afternoons, they explored the cliffs. On the final day of their stay they rented horses and rode along the top of the cliffs that looked down on the Bay of Morecombe.

They rode for two hours, then dismounted and ate the picnic the hotel had packed. After he had eaten, Daniel yawned and said he needed a nap. With his distinctive grace, he stretched out on the grass, confided his head to Anne's lap, and promptly went to sleep.

Anne looked down at his perfect face, then up at the tranquil blue sky. The only sounds she heard were the calling of the birds and the splashes the little waves made as they broke on the shingle of the narrow beach below.

Her heart was bursting with happiness. She had never dreamed it was possible to be so happy. She had never dreamed it was possible to feel this way about a man. She closed her eyes and said a prayer that nothing would change, that Daniel would love her forever, as she would love him.

*

They checked out of the hotel in the morning, got into the rented carriage, and were driven toward home.

"I wish we could have stayed longer," Anne said wistfully as the carriage rolled out of the small town.

"It's not possible to escape the real world forever," Daniel said practically. "I'm sure you miss your animals, and I need to get back to work on the factory. The main building is finished, but I can't hire workers until the cottages are done."

Anne hesitated, then decided it was safe to ask. "I've always wondered why you wanted to build a cotton factory, Daniel. I know you brought a lot of money home from India, so why do something like this? You must know it won't help you establish yourself in society."

He was sitting close beside her and when she finished speaking he didn't move, but she had the definite impression that in some way he had withdrawn. He said crisply, "I built it to provide jobs for people who don't have any, and to prove that you can provide your workers with a living wage, a decent place to live and still make money for yourself."

Anne was already sorry she had asked, but now she was committed. She said softly, "I understand that people need jobs. I saw it in London—little girls trying to sell flowers, little boys sweeping manure off the crossings. It was terribly sad, and it was one of the reasons I didn't like London. We don't have poverty like that in the country."

He regarded her with one raised black eyebrow. "You most certainly do have poverty, my dear. Do you have any idea how many small factories in Lancashire have been closed? When the war ended the owners had nowhere to sell their goods, so they just shut down and put all of their employees out of work." The blue eyes held hers pitilessly. "Do you know how many 'country people' are going hungry because of the enclosure laws?"

He seemed to expect an answer so Anne shook her head slightly, afraid to speak.

"Do you know anything about the enclosure laws, Anne?"

He had called her Anne, not Annie. She deeply regretted that she had asked about the factory, but there was no way she could get out of the conversation now. She scoured her memory and answered hesitantly, "Didn't they have something to do with the government's taking common land away from the people who were using it and giving it to larger farmers?"

"My dear, the enclosure laws have everything to do with the government taking common land away from the laborers and small farmers to whom it had always belonged. Can you possibly understand how important—how vital—it is for poor people to have access to a piece of land? They can grow their own crops on common land, and they can graze a pig or a goat. But when the enclosure laws virtually confiscated the commonly held land from the people who worked it, all of those small farmers and agricultural laborers no longer had the means to feed their families."

Anne was starting to pay closer attention to what he was saying. "But what did these people do, Daniel? How did they survive?"

"The mill owners hired them, paid them a pittance, and left them to live in misery. Factory owners made fortunes on the backs of the poor devils, forcing them to work under conditions I wouldn't wish on a dog."

Anne was becoming upset. "I didn't know about this. When Papa is home he has a London paper delivered to the house, but I never really looked at it. I was too busy reading books in the library that had little to do with what was happening in the world I lived in."

He said ruefully, "I don't mean to blame you, Annie. There's absolutely no reason why you should know about such things. But these mill workers live at the lowest level of the population, with no education or sanitation. Most of the men are subjected to long hours and demoralizing drudgery. It's no wonder that the level of drunkenness among them is so high. I built my factory to demonstrate that it's possible to make money and treat your workers well at the same time."

One thing puzzled Anne. "Daniel, you were just a boy when you went out to India. How do you come to know so much about working conditions in England?"

"He leaned his back against the coach cushion and looked straight ahead. "I wasn't that young when I left for India, and I had seen the enclosure results in my own village. Families I knew, boys I knew…there were no jobs for them, and without jobs there was no money and no food. And in India? Well, let me just say that the discrepancy between the well off and the poor was even greater. They have castes there, Annie, and the differences between the rich and the poor are unchanging and perpetual. It's simply not moral."

She was silent, digesting what he had said, when he turned to her with an ironic smile. "I had big plans at sixteen. I was going to make a fortune in India and come back to England to save all my friends and the people like them."

She reached out and took his hand. "Isn't that precisely what you're doing?"

His smile was wry. "One factory seems like a handful of sand thrown on the desert."

"It won't be that to the people who work there. And perhaps it will become a model that others will follow."

"That is what I'm hoping for. I've met a few like-minded men in government, and that's encouraging."

She lifted his hand to her lips and kissed it. "Your factory will be a beacon of light, both to the poor and to those who want to see social conditions in the country change. It probably won't happen overnight, but it will happen. I'm certain of it, Daniel."

His gave her his wonderful smile, slid closer and put his arm around her shoulders. "Thank you for saying that, Annie. I'm glad you understand."

Anne nestled her head into his shoulder and closed her eyes. "You're welcome," she said, and fell asleep against the warmth of his body.

CHAPTER TWELVE

The newly married couple did not return to a peaceful home. There were workmen in the house and workmen in the stable. Since Daniel wanted Amit brought to Grex as soon as possible, he removed a number of carpenters from the house to build a stall sturdy enough to hold a breeding stallion.

To Anne's secret amusement, the house carpenters adored Miss Bonteen. "I can't believe how much work you've got out of them while we were gone, Bonny!" she had said with admiration when first she saw the energetic workforce.

"It took me awhile to find what I needed to do to keep them going," her gentle friend said.

"And what is that?" Anne asked with genuine curiosity.

"I feed them. They have a tea break every hour, and then they get back to work. They think I'm incredibly generous to give them so much time to eat, but when I calculated how much time they were taking when left to themselves, we are getting considerably more work done."

Anne was still laughing when she finished. "Good for you, Bonny." she said.

"Unfortunately, with Mr. Dereham taking half my workers away, the house project will slow down."

"Don't fret, Bonny. We have comfortable bedrooms to retire to and it's important we do the same for the horses."

Bonnie sighed. "It's always about the horses."

Anne laughed again.

*

Daniel's stallion and two mares finally came, accompanied by an Indian groom. This unusual individual provoked astonishment from Anne's two stable workers. Both Frankie, who was quite old, and Timmy, who was quite young, had lived near Grex for their entire lives, and never thought they'd set eyes upon a genuine turban-wearing Indian.

"It's hard to understand him, my lady," Frankie complained the day after Kumar arrived. "He seems to think he's speaking English, but he ain't."

"You're all horsemen," Anne said encouragingly to the duo confronting her. "That's a common language all over the world. I'm sure you can make yourselves understood."

Frankie had to admit that the bloke had taken wonderful care of Mr. Dereham's horses. "They're beautiful, my lady, that I will give him. Two beautiful, beautiful mares! And the stallion! He's full of fire, that boy."

"They're pure Arabians, Frankie. Our thoroughbreds originated with an Arabian, you know."

"Aye, my lady. That I do know." He heaved a resigned sigh. "I supposed we'll manage, my lady. We always have."

"Thank you, Frankie," Anne said. "I knew I could count on you."

*

Anne was still in love, but not quite so mindlessly happy as she had been on her honeymoon. There was so much about Daniel that was unknown territory. She knew nothing about his parents, about where he was born, about anything concrete in his life before she had married him. She didn't even know his birthday!

She, on the other hand, was an open book. Her life could be summed up in a few lines:

Born at Grex in Yorkshire, England, on February 28, 1798. Only daughter of the Earl of Grex.

Married to Mr. Daniel Dereham on May 18, 1817.

She had yet to produce children to add to that biography, but when she did, that would be the summary of her life.

She could not create even so simple a summary as that for Daniel. He had told her he was 26, so he must have been born in 1791. She knew he had run away from home and gone to India when he was 16. She knew he had come home from India with a fortune. That was it.

She had asked him about his parents once. It was while they were lying in bed after making love. His arm was lying lightly over her breasts, and she had turned to him and asked softly, "You never mention your parents, Daniel. Are they still alive?"

She felt his arm stiffen. Then he took it away. "As far as I know." His voice was chillingly indifferent.

"You mean…you don't know?"

"That is precisely what I meant," he returned. "You don't think I ran off to India because of my happy home life, do you Anne?"

"I see," Anne said.

He turned, presenting her with a view of his bare muscled back. "Now, if you don't mind, I'm going to sleep. It's very late and we have a lot to do tomorrow."

Anne had never again asked him about his family, but he had succeeded in engaging her curiosity. She knew that who Daniel was had a lot to do with where he came from, and she wondered if it might be possible for her to find out about him some other way.

*

After Daniel was certain his horses had settled in, he decided to pay a visit to the factory. "I'll be gone only a few days," he told Anne. "The gas must be in by now, and I want to see how it's working."

As he drove his curricle away from Grex, Daniel reflected on the last month of his life. He was pleased with his marriage. Anne had been a nice surprise. She was lovely to look at, with her great dark eyes, long slender neck, dark hair and ivory coloring. He liked to watch her as she moved—her waist was slender and supple, her legs long and slim. Altogether, she had turned out to be thoroughly satisfactory.

Daniel was not thinking about Anne, however, as his carriage reached the outskirts of Manchester, where his factory was located.

Dusk was falling as he drove up the new road, the factory rising before him. It was eight stories high, with forty windows on each of its long sides and twenty windows on its shorter sides. In order to accommodate the power looms, each floor had been built with twelve-foot high ceilings, so all of the windows were very tall. And right now, every one of them was blazing with light. A beacon of the future, Daniel hoped.

He had planned on using gas from the moment he broke ground. It had taken time and money to have the lines brought in, but gas was safer than any other option. Cheaper too. The Napoleonic and American wars had cut down the supply of whale oil and tallow, which had pushed the price of lamp oil and candles sky high. Gas, Daniel firmly believed, was the way of the future.

He drove his horses into what looked like a small village, with streets laid out in rectangular form, all of them lined with wooden cottages. Daniel drove down the main street and pulled up at the only cottage that looked occupied. A man came out the front door as Daniel stopped his horses. "I didn't know when you were coming," Robert Denver said.

"I had some things to settle at home," Daniel replied.

Denver went to the horses' heads and Daniel jumped down from the curricle. He joined his friend and the both of them stood still, looking at the lighted factory.

"The gas looks wonderful," Daniel said.

"That it does. They finally finished putting it in—it took them long enough. I turned it on tonight so I could admire it. You came at just the right time."

"Let's take a look at the houses," Daniel said after they had gazed their fill. The workers' cottages had all been built on a similar plan. They had a sitting room, a dining room and a kitchen on the first floor, all with fireplaces. Upstairs some cottages had four bedrooms and some had five, making them considerably larger than the usual two up and two down inhabited by most country people. They also had a patch of land in the back for a garden. The smell of fresh wood permeated the air of the cottage that Daniel and Denver chose to inspect.

"The families who move in here are going to think they're in heaven," Denver said, as he and Daniel went from room to room.

"Children deserve to live in decent surroundings," Daniel said firmly. "I believe the children who live in these houses will grow up to be the kind of people we need for the future."

"You've certainly invested a ton of money to make that happen," Denver said.

"I'll make it back, and more."

Denver smiled. "If anyone can do it, you can Daniel."

The two men went back outside and stopped to look at the glowing factory again. Then Daniel punched his friend lightly on the shoulder and said, "Do you think my factory manager might offer me a drink?"

"Come along," Denver said with a grin. "I think I might have a wee bit of something in the house."

CHAPTER THIRTEEN

Summer passed and the work on the house and stables continued. The servants' quarters were in the attic under the roof, and even though most of the roof was finished, the bedrooms needed to be renovated. While the bedrooms were being worked on, the servants lived on the third floor in rooms that would normally be reserved for guests. This meant Anne could accommodate only a few servants.

She had engaged a butler, two footmen, a cook and a scullery maid. Daniel was without a valet and Anne without a lady's maid. If she needed help dressing, she knew she could always call on Bonny, and Daniel was used to doing for himself. The large crew of workmen lived in the village or paid to stay in local homes. Daniel paid the bill for all the rentals.

By the time October came around the stable was finished. At the moment it lodged Amit, Daniel's two Arabian mares and the two carriage horses. Anne also had Molly and Tucker and a lovely young thoroughbred gelding that Daniel had surprised her with. She had named him Bonfire because of his bright chestnut coloring.

"The stable is cozier than the house is right now," Anne remarked to Daniel as they walked together around the unoccupied paddocks to see what else could be done before the weather changed.

"At least the ceilings won't fall on us and most of the roof is finished," Daniel said. "We have a few nice rooms to live in and the kitchen is almost done. The men can carry on with the inside work throughout the winter."

"We'll survive," Anne said cheerfully.

He smiled at her. "Thank God for your sweet disposition, Annie. Most women would be distraught living in a house that is filled with dust and noise."

"I'm so happy to see Grex coming to life again that I believe I could tolerate almost anything."

She wanted to say, "As long as I have you, I can tolerate anything." But she didn't say it. She knew the parts of him he showed to her, the tender lover, the dedicated horseman, the socially conscious factory owner. But so much about him was still unknown. He had a desk in the library that was piled high with letters and communications from a vast array of banks and solicitors and businessmen in London, but he never received a personal letter. They never spoke of anything outside the horses, the renovations on Grex, and—because she was truly interested—he kept her current with what was happening with the factory.

It was at full employment, he told her. The cottages were filled with laborers and their families, and the weaving was going smoothly. No one worked more than eight hours a day. Daniel's famous or infamous phrase, depending upon the mindset of the speaker, was: eight hours work, eight hours recreation and eight hours sleep. He did not employ women or children. Nor was it necessary for them to work, as the men made enough to keep their families comfortable. And, even with the outflow of money on salaries and upkeep, Daniel was on track to recoup his initial investment and make money.

One chilly late fall afternoon Anne and Daniel were walking back to the house with Dorothy trotting at Anne's heels. They had been discussing the prospect of taking over the home farm again, when they passed Amit's paddock. The stallion had been separated from the mares by the carriage horses and Anne's horses, and he was restless in the energizing cold air. When he saw Daniel, he whinnied and came galloping up to the stone wall that separated him from the road.

"What's this all about, eh?" Daniel asked, as he went over to the horse. "I gave you a good ride this morning."

Amit threw up his head and galloped to the far side of the paddock, showing them his back. Once there he looked over his shoulder at Daniel, and Daniel grinned. "He's so conceited," he said to Anne, his voice filled with affection. "He thinks the world revolves around him."

Amit came trotting back to them, his head held high, his black mane blowing, his tail floating behind him, and Anne laughed. "He is conceited, true. But he has a lot to be conceited about."

Daniel rubbed the stallion's arched neck, and then he and Anne continued their walk back to the house, chatting companionably.

*

Two days later Anne and Miss Bonteen were measuring the parlor floor so Anne could order a new rug, when the butler, Thornton, came to the doorway. Anne, who had just finished writing down the dimensions Miss Bonteen was reading out, looked up and said, "Yes, Thornton?"

"My lady, someone has called to see Mr. Dereham."

This had never happened before. "I see," Anne said, trying not to show her surprise. "Did you find out who it is?

"Yes, my lady." The butler's face was immobile. "He gave his name as Mr. Owen Dereham. He said he was Mr. Dereham's father."

"His father?" Anne said in a shocked voice.

"That is what he said, my lady."

Miss Bonteen said, "I will go to the door and speak to him, Anne. If he is indeed who he says he is…"

Anne said faintly, "Thank you Bonny. You had better bring him in here."

Miss Bonteen followed Thornton out of the room.

Anne stood, clutching her notebook in her hand. She didn't know what to think, but she had an instinct that this sudden appearance from the past would not please Daniel.

She was still frozen in the middle of the room when she heard the sound of footsteps coming down the hall. Miss Bonteen came into the room first, followed by a sturdy-looking man dressed neatly in the kind of clothing the local farmers wore when going to church. His hair was light brown, his shoulders were wide and he looked to be in his fifties.

He looked nothing like Daniel.

Anne rallied. "How do you do, Mr. Dereham. I am Daniel's wife, Anne. I fear my husband is not available at the moment, but if you care to wait he should be with us shortly."

"Thank you ma'am," the strange man said.

"This is Lady Anne," Miss Bonteen said sharply, in objection to the plebian ma'am.

"Sorry," the man said, not seeming embarrassed by the correction. "Lady Anne."

"Won't you come in and have a seat?" Anne asked. "I was just going to send for tea."

"Thank you, ma...Lady Anne. A cup of tea would taste real good. I've had a bit of a drive and my horse is weary and hungry as well."

Anne looked at Miss Bonteen. That lady promptly said, "I'll go and make sure Mr. Dereham's horse is being taken care of, my dear."

"Thank you, Bonny. And will you tell Thornton we would like some tea."

"Of course," Miss Bonteen replied.

Anne gestured to the blue velvet armchair that was placed at right angles to the sofa. "Please, Mr. Dereham, make yourself comfortable. Tea should be here shortly."

The man went to the chair and Anne seated herself on the sofa, turning to face her guest. He had a farmer's face, brown from the sun, with wrinkles at the corners of his hazel eyes. His broad, stocky body looked strong and muscular.

Anne said, "Is Daniel expecting you, Mr. Dereham?"

The man gave a short laugh. "No, he is not, Lady Anne."

"I see," Anne said, who didn't.

The tea tray came in and Anne was grateful for the ceremony of tea pouring to provide a little conversation. She had no idea what she could—or should—say to this man who claimed to be her husband's father.

She took a sip of her tea and said, in some desperation, "Your arrival will be a surprise to Daniel, then?"

"I'm damn certain it will be a surprise." The man who claimed to be Daniel's father returned his cup to its saucer with a clink. "That laddie has a lot to answer for to his mother, and that's what I've come to tell him."

"Is his mother all right?" Anne asked.

"She is, and no thanks to him. She's worried herself sick for ten years, and now he's back in the country—for over a year!—and he doesn't send a word to her. Not a single word! Well, I'm here to set him straight on what his duty is, Lady Anne, whether he likes it or no."

Anne stared at Daniel's father in fascinated horror. What on earth is Daniel going to do when he sees him? When he hears him?

Mr. Dereham's face relaxed a trifle as he looked at her. "I'm sorry to swear in your own sitting room, Lady Anne. But I'm that angry with the lad…"

Anne, whose ears had been alert for a sound in the hallway, heard it now. Footsteps. Daniel's footsteps. She would know that light tread anywhere.

The door opened and Daniel came into the room. Mr. Dereham stood up and the two men faced each other. Daniel's face was white and his eyes were blazing.

"What are you doing here?" His voice was pitched low but it reverberated with anger.

"I'm here to tell you to come and visit your mother," Mr. Dereham said. Then, unsteadily, "Christ, lad, but it's good to see you."

"I'm afraid I can't return the compliment," Daniel replied icily.

"For God's sake, lad, you're not sixteen anymore! You're a grown man, not the boy who ran away to India because he heard

93

something he didn't like. You broke your mother's heart when you left, did you know that?"

Daniel's expression didn't change. "She knows why I left. You know why I left. Nothing has changed since I took ship for India ten years ago. You knew I was safe—once I was established I sent you money every month. I'm still sending you money..."

"We don't want your damned money!" Mr. Dereham took a few steps toward his son. "We want you to come home and visit us! Your mother is longing to see you. Come back with me. You know how much she loves you..."

Daniel held up his hand. His color had returned and his expression was bleak. "If she loved me so much she shouldn't have lied to me. You can stay here the night then return home in the morning."

For the first time since he had come in, Daniel looked at Anne. "I'm going out to the factory for a few days. Give him some food and a bed, but I want him gone in the morning. Do you understand?"

Speechless, Anne managed a nod.

Daniel turned and strode out of the room, closing the door behind him.

Anne stared at the closed door, then slowly turned to look at her guest. He looked almost as furious as Daniel. She said quietly, "I'm very sorry, Mr. Dereham. I've never seen Daniel so upset. I'm sure he'll get over it." She wasn't sure at all, but she had to say something.

Dereham collapsed into his chair as if he hadn't the strength to stay on his feet. As Anne watched him, his anger drained away to be replaced by sadness. "Damn stubborn youngster," he said, as if to himself. "I thought, after all those years in a foreign land, he'd be ready to see his mother again." He thrust his hand through his hair. "God, what am I going to tell Maria? Her heart will be broke a second time."

Anne felt totally out of her depth. "Perhaps if you give Daniel a little more time?" she ventured.

He looked at her as if he had forgot she was there. "Oh, Lady Anne." He sighed. "Don't worry, I won't be trespassing on your hospitality for the night. I can easily find an inn for me and the horse."

"Absolutely not," Anne said decisively. She was not letting this man get away; she had too much she wanted to ask him. "I will have a bedroom made up for you, and don't worry about dressing for dinner. We don't bother half the time. As you will notice, the house is under construction."

Dereham relaxed. "Thank you, lass. If you don't mind, I could rightly use a wee drop of whiskey right now."

"Of course."

Anne rang the bell and Thornton came in. Anne gave the order and the butler returned promptly with a crystal decanter and glass on a tray. When Dereham had finished his whiskey, Anne looked at his weary face and decided to hold her questions for dinner.

"You look tired," she said sympathetically. "I'll show you to your room myself. We dine at seven, so you'll have time for a little rest."

"Thank you, Lady Anne." He rose to his feet. "I was hoping for a happier outcome to my journey."

Anne felt sorry for the man. In truth, she had been deeply shocked by Daniel's behavior. What could have happened between Daniel and his mother to have provoked him, at the age of sixteen, to leave his family and his country for India? Anne planned to do all she could to find out the answer to this puzzle before Daniel's father left for home tomorrow.

CHAPTER FOURTEEN

Anne asked Miss Bonteen if she would mind having her dinner in her room. "I hate to do this to you, Bonny, but I need to ask Mr. Dereham some personal questions and I think he might be more forthcoming if it was just me he was speaking to."

Miss Bonteen understood, as she always did, and Anne went down to dinner in her afternoon dress, still trying to think of tactful ways to get the information she wanted. She and Daniel always dined in the breakfast room as the dining room was closed off until the ceiling could be replaced. Since it was only Daniel and Anne and Miss Bonteen who ate there, all of the leaves had been taken out of the table making it much easier to converse. There was a buffet in the room with some crystal adorning the polished mahogany top (the family silver had been sold long ago), and one of the few decent Persian rugs in the house was on the floor. Anne had found a nice picture of the countryside in the attic, and that hung on the wall.

Anne thought the room was pleasantly simple, but when Mr. Dereham joined her, he looked uncomfortable. He said, "I don't need to take my supper in such grand surroundings, Lady Anne. A cup of soup and some bread in my room would be grand."

Anne smiled. "Nonsense. I expect Daniel's father to eat with the family, and we are family now, aren't we?"

He gave her a rueful smile. "That's not the way Daniel sees it, I'm afraid." He seated himself next to her, where a place had been laid, and took a long drink of water.

"I will be frank with you, Mr. Dereham," Anne said. "Daniel has been silent about his life before he went to India. I am hoping you might help to explain him to me."

"A mystery, is he?"

"Yes. And not just to me. He came home from India with this huge fortune, and no one knows how he got it. And no one knows where he came from, or who his people are."

"And he hasn't told you, lass?" Mr. Dereham's sun-creased face looked surprised.

"He hasn't told me anything. And anytime I've tried to ask, he puts a No Trespassing sign up so fast that I can only back away. I didn't even know he had a mother and father still living."

Silence fell as Thornton brought the soup in. He placed it in front of them then left the room as was his custom. Daniel didn't like servants hanging about when he was dining with Anne.

Mr. Dereham took a spoonful of the soup. "This is very good," he said.

"Thank you. Mrs. Marsh does a nice oxtail soup."

Anne took a spoonful of soup as well.

Silence fell again and Anne made no attempt to break it. When the soup was finished, she rang the bell and Jeremy came in to remove the soup bowls, and Thornton carried in the roast, potatoes and a large platter of vegetables.

"Thank you, Thornton," Anne said. "We'll serve ourselves."

Mr. Dereham looked at the large roast and smiled. "Daniel has done well for himself if he can afford food like this for only two people."

Anne made no reply, but smiled back and spooned some vegetables onto her plate.

Mr. Dereham said, "I suppose I had better tell you what you want to know. It's not right that Daniel should keep his wife in the dark."

"It would be a great kindness. I care a great deal for Daniel, Mr. Dereham, and I know he carries pain inside him."

He sighed. "Yes, lass, I'm sorry to say he has pain, and even sorrier to admit his mother and I are the cause of it." He put his spoon down and regarded her gravely. "We made a bad mistake. We let Daniel grow up thinking he was my son, and when he found out the truth he was angry. Very angry—with me, but more so with his mother. They were always very close—he was her only child—

and when he found out she had been lying to him, he was hurt. Bitterly hurt. He demanded to know the name of his real father, and she wouldn't tell him. He said some ugly things to her, which had her in tears. Then I jumped in and told him if he couldn't speak decently to his mother then he wasn't welcome in my house."

He gave Anne a weary look. "If only I'd have kept my big mouth shut, perhaps everything would have settled down. But I said what I said, and Daniel flung himself out of the house, slamming the door behind him. I fully expected him to come back once he had calmed down, but the next we heard he had signed on to a ship that was sailing to India. We haven't heard a word from him since."

Anne's heart was wrung. For Daniel because of how he had found out the truth about his parentage. But also, for his mother and this good man, both of whom had lost their only son. "I'm so sorry," she said softly. "I am so sorry, Mr. Dereham. But Daniel isn't that sixteen-year-old boy any more. Surely, if you give him time, he'll come around."

"He may not be sixteen, but all of those boyish feelings of hurt and betrayal are still smoldering inside him. I saw that today."

Anne had seen it too, and while her heart ached for her husband, she could not help but feel compassion for his mother. "Why was he so angry at his mother?" she asked. "Shouldn't he have been more angry with you?"

"As I said before, he and Maria were very close. He looks very like her, except for the eyes. Hers are brown—like yours."

"Did other people who knew you suspect the truth?"

He shook his head. "Maria and I had known each other when we were youngsters. Then she went into service with some English earl. It was supposed to be a great opportunity for her. She came back home a year later, unmarried and carrying a child."

Anne, who had been prepared to hear this, murmured, "Poor girl."

He gave her a grateful smile. "That's not the way our neighborhood would have seen it. Maria would have been excluded from village life, and her child would have been bullied and excluded by the local children. Her mother knew that and she came to my mother and told her how her daughter had been attacked by one of the big lords after a drunken party and ended up pregnant. She begged my mother to ask me to marry Maria.

"And that is how it happened. My mam asked me if I would, and I consented. I was of age to be married, but none of the local girls interested me. I think my mother agreed because she was afraid I was never going to marry at all."

"Still," Anne said, "under the circumstances it was very kind of you to do such a thing."

He shrugged. "Maria was a good girl. She didn't deserve such a terrible thing to happen to her. So we married and we told everyone Daniel was born early. It was a hard birth, though, and the doctor told Maria she could have no more children."

He paused, and Anne said softly, "That must have been hard on you. You would never have a son of your own."

He shook his head. "I never thought that way. Daniel was such a joy. So loving, so smart, so talented. He fell in love with horses when he was seven years old. Did he tell you that, lass?"

"He hasn't told me anything, Mr. Dereham," Anne said.

"He used to ride my plow horses. He looked so comical, this skinny little boy perched on top of the huge horse, but those horses would do anything for him. It was amazing, really. Then, when he was twelve, the squire asked if he would exercise his two race horses. Daniel was in heaven. He rode the horses while the squire had them at home, and then, when the squire took them to the racetrack, Daniel went along. One time, at the last minute the squire's jockey got sick, and Daniel ended up riding in the race. He won. He was thirteen."

Mr. Dereham's face was bright with pride. "That lad could do anything with horses. The squire had two horses and one of them—

the one Daniel rode—was turning out to be quite good. So the squire hired Daniel to be his groom and his jockey."

"Did he go to school at all?" Anne asked.

"Aye, he went to the village school until he was ten. He was so smart. The teacher told us he was way ahead of the other children.

"Did the other children resent him?

"Na. Everyone wanted to be friends with Daniel."

Anne said slowly, "I expect he felt as if his life had been pulled out from under him when he heard he wasn't who he thought he was."

"Aye, I fear that was it. And I think he would have come around if he hadn't done such a damn fool thing as getting on a ship to India! We didn't hear a word from him for two years. His poor mam was beside herself. Then we started to get money. It was drawn on an English bank, but I managed to find out that it was coming from India. Well, it had to be Daniel, didn't it? We didn't want the money, but we were relieved to hear he was alive."

Neither of them had taken a bite of their food. Mr. Dereham glanced at his plate and said, "Here now, I don't want to insult your cook by sending this back uneaten."

"I'm so sorry—I've kept you from your dinner. Please take your time, Mr. Dereham. There's no rush."

He began to eat and Anne put her fork through a slice of beef, then let it rest on her plate. She couldn't eat a thing. She was too upset by what she had heard.

Poor Daniel, she thought. His father was right. If he had only remained in England he would most probably have got over the shock. But he went to a strange country and let it fester inside him.

Of course, if he had remained in England, Anne would never have met or married him, and she couldn't wish for that. She needed to think of some way she could help him overcome this anger. She pictured her husband's face in her mind and wondered how on earth she was going to manage that.

CHAPTER FIFTEEN

Daniel spent three days at the factory walking around and speaking to his employees and their families. One of the things he mentioned to the wives was his plan to build a school for their children. Daniel had been fortunate enough to be sent to a village school. Most of the children he knew had not been so privileged. If he had not been literate and mathematically competent, Daniel knew he would never have won so high a place at the maharajah's court. This experience had contributed to his belief that an education was essential if an individual wanted to climb out of poverty.

When he told the gathered wives about his proposed school, they were first stunned, then overjoyed. Since their husbands' wages were enough to keep the family, their children did not need to work, so the opportunity to attend school was realistic. Daniel explained that it would be necessary to first build a schoolhouse and find teachers, but when the school opened the opportunity to attend would be available to all their children.

"Thank you, Mr. Dereham!" said Mrs. Evans, the woman who had gathered the group for Daniel. "And thank you for building this clean, safe factory for our men to work in. And for providing such nice living quarters. We pray for you all the time, we do." She turned to the women surrounding her.

"Aye, that we do," came the chorused reply.

"Sure and you're a saint, Mr. Dereham," an Irish voice called from the back of the group.

Daniel looked at the careworn faces of these women and felt a lump come into his throat. The factory had been an idea in his head for so long that it had become almost an abstraction. The people he was trying to help had become abstractions too. But now, as he looked at these women, so many of them with babes in their arms and little ones at their skirts, the reality was personal once more.

He said, "I'm no saint, ladies. This factory isn't a charity. I plan to make quite a lot of money from this venture."

"I hope you do!" came another voice from the back of the delegation.

All of the women laughed.

Daniel said, "I thank you for that thought, and for coming to see me. And I promise you will have your school."

He was thinking of this scene as he rode home the following day. Before the school could be built and staffed, he needed to find someone who shared his beliefs to organize it. He couldn't ask Robbie Denver. Robbie had enough to do managing the factory. He supposed he'd have to rely on the employment agencies in London to find someone qualified.

As the miles dropped away and he drew closer to home, the memory of what had sent him tearing off crept insistently into his mind. He had pushed it aside while he was at the factory, but he wasn't going to be able to ignore it forever.

He had been stunned to see his father—his stepfather—sitting cozily in the parlor at Grex. Seeing that familiar face brought back all the turmoil and anger he had felt when last they met. He had made a life for himself without them—a good life! He didn't want anything or anyone to stir the embers of a fire he had hoped was quenched.

He thought of Anne and felt a little sick. What had she thought? What had his father told her?

Daniel did not want his wife to know about his past. She had accepted him as he was. She loved him as he was. He didn't want to upset a marriage that had turned out to be so agreeable. He didn't want Anne asking questions about his life before they met.

*

Anne had thought of nothing but Daniel since he rode away in a cloud of fury. She knew what it was like to be betrayed by a parent, to find out the people you trusted were not what you thought they were. But she had come to terms with it. Daniel, on the other hand, had never come to terms with it. The wound had festered inside him until it devoured his memories of the love and devotion he had received from his mother and stepfather.

She worried about what she should do when Daniel returned. Should she confront him and try to make him see reason? He needed to get beyond the duplicity of his parents and see them for what they were—two people who loved him very much. It had been clear to Anne that when he fled to India he had hurt them as much as they hurt him.

The more Anne thought about the situation, the more she thought it would be best to hold her tongue. Daniel had to confide in her before she could help him. She had a feeling that if she were the one to bring up the subject of his parents, it would drive him away.

Anne was only nineteen, but her life had made her wiser than her age. She knew what it was like to be betrayed, and she knew what it was to be lonely, and because of these experiences she was able to understand her husband. When he made love to her, she felt that he was with her, part of her in more than just the physical way. But the barriers came back as soon as normal life resumed.

So when he came riding home after his precipitous departure, she greeted him with a smile and made no mention of his stepfather's visit. They sat down to dinner without Miss Bonteen, who was paying a visit in the village, and Daniel told Anne about his idea for a school.

"The simple fact is that a person who cannot read or write or do sums cannot rise out of poverty." The expression on his face was intensely serious. "If we want to eliminate poverty in this country, we must send children to school. It's as simple as that."

Anne said, "It's a wonderful idea, Daniel. I'm so proud of you for thinking of it."

He smiled at her over the rim of his wine glass. "Thank you, Annie, but I'm not a hero. An educated, informed populace benefits all of society."

She leaned a little toward him. "What are your plans for making the school a reality?"

He put his glass down. "I'm going to have to find someone qualified to do it for me. I can't ask Robbie, he's too busy with the factory. Besides he knows as little as I do about the needs of a new school."

Suddenly Anne's young face lit to radiance. "Daniel, I have an idea! Bonny and I can build this school. Bonny actually taught in a school before she came to be my governess, so she is the perfect person to take this on! And I can help her!"

She looked so beautiful as she leaned toward him in her eagerness. But he didn't like the idea. He didn't like the idea of her spending time near the factory. Her cheeks were flushed and her eyes were sparkling. He didn't want to start an argument now. He had plans for her this evening that depended upon her being in a good mood. He said temperately, "We'll discuss it later, Annie. Right now, I'd like to talk about what you've been doing while I was gone. How are the horses?"

Conversation flowed until dinner was finished and they went into the drawing room for tea.

*

Daniel said he was tired and Anne was happy to retire early. They were no sooner in bed together, however, when he reached for her. She laughed and asked him what had happened to his tiredness. His answer was to kiss her, and she responded as she always had, with generosity and trust.

Daniel had never been anything but gentle with his young bride, but tonight she felt a difference. Tonight, his hands were hard, his face was hard, and there were very few caresses before he moved over her and into her. She felt the urgency in him, the desperation, and she didn't stiffen against him. Instead she put her arms around him and yielded to the raw need that was driving him.

When he had finished and was lying on his back next to her, his breathing coming hard and fast, she put her head on his shoulder and nestled against him. "You certainly didn't act tired," she said softly.

His arm came up to encircle her. "I'm sorry, Annie. I don't know what came over me. I just… I'm sorry. You didn't deserve that."

She didn't answer.

He rested his cheek against her hair. After a long quiet moment he said, "Your hair always smells so good. Like the springtime."

She smiled, turned her head, gently kissed his bare chest and said, "I'm glad you don't have a lot of hair on your body."

She could feel his body relax. "I don't deserve you," he said.

"That's probably true," she replied.

He chuckled.

Anne closed her eyes and snuggled her head a bit deeper into his shoulder.

He said in a constricted voice, "About what happened the other day…"

"Mmmm?" she murmured.

"Did my father, my stepfather, did he tell you what happened? I mean did he tell you why I left home?"

"He did." Anne held herself very still while trying to keep her body relaxed.

"What did you think?" He sounded young and uncertain—not like Daniel at all.

"I think you felt they had betrayed you."

"Yes!" Now he sounded like himself. "For my whole life they let me think the man who acted as my father was my father. They lied. For years and years and years, they lied."

She said carefully, not wanting him to reject her now that he was finally opening up, "Do you think their love was a lie?"

There was a long silence. Anne kept very still, her cheek against his warm shoulder. Finally, he said, in a voice that sounded almost sad, "No. I don't think that."

She didn't say anything and for a long time they remained quiet, her head on his shoulder. When he moved she thought he was going to say it was time to go to sleep, but instead he asked, "Do you want to hear how I found out the truth?"

CHAPTER SIXTEEN

Anne's heartbeat accelerated. "If you want to tell me."

He touched his lips to her hair and began to speak. "When I was a boy I used to ride horses for our local squire. He had a few thoroughbreds that he raced, and I would exercise them when they were at home. When I got older I began to ride them in actual races. I loved it. The horses weren't top o' the line, but they were willing, and we often placed in the top three.

"The closest racetrack wasn't one of the big, famous ones, but it had one historic race that attracted top trainers and breeders every year. Squire Masterson rarely raced his horses that day—they weren't in the same class as the horses that came in for the Esham Cup. Even though I had no ride, I always went to the track with a few friends to watch. This one time—the year that everything happened—everything seemed as usual. We stood around the rail and watched, while all the fine folk watched from their carriages. We were all waiting for the big race, which would be run last. Then, in the race directly before the Cup, one of the riders took a nasty fall and broke his arm. Obviously, he could no longer ride, and he was scheduled as second call on a horse that was running in the Cup. The owner and trainer, faced with their injured jockey, started looking around for someone else to ride.

"All of the regular jockeys were already engaged to ride, and it was looking as if the horse would have to be pulled. Someone must have suggested me because Mr. Fogarty, one of the important trainers, came to find me and asked me to ride his horse. The horse was Malabas, Annie. The favorite! I don't know if I was excited or scared—probably a bit of both—but of course I said yes.

"Mr. Fogarty grabbed my arm and began to steer me toward where the horses were waiting to be saddled. 'Come and meet the Earl of Preston, Malabas' owner,' he said. 'If he's all right with you, then you'll ride. And I hope to God you're as good as all these locals swear you are.'"

"We wove our way through the crowd and finally fetched up beside a gorgeous bay thoroughbred. He had to be seventeen hands high, Annie! Then a man stepped forward and said, 'So this is the local wonder who is good enough to ride my horse.'

"'So they say, my lord,' Mr. Fogarty answered. 'I suggest we put him up and see how he handles the horse before we make a decision.'"

"The earl came over to me. He was tall and thin and he grabbed my chin and turned my face up to his, saying, 'Do you think you can do this boy?' I looked up at him."

Daniel's arm tightened around her, as if he wanted to make sure she was still there. He continued in a voice that trembled slightly, "Annie, it was almost like looking into a mirror. He had the exact same eyes as mine! They were the exact same blue and had that same peculiar frosted look. I've never seen them on anyone else. Yet there they were, looking down at me, the same color, the same black eyelashes, the same curve of eyebrow."

Anne saw where this was leading and her heart began to thump.

Daniel continued, "He went white as chalk, Annie. Then he shoved me—he shoved me so hard I almost fell!—and he said to Fogarty, 'Get this brat out of my sight! I never want to see him again!'"

A shudder went through him as he repeated those words, and the arm that held her to him tightened even more.

"Dear God," she breathed. "Dear God in heaven."

They lay together in silence. Daniel's arm was like a vise around her, but Anne hardly noticed. She said at last, "Is he your real father, Daniel?"

"He has to be. If he weren't, why would he have reacted so violently when he saw me? He recognized me, and he wanted nothing to do with me."

Anne tried to think of a word bad enough to describe the Earl of Preston and came up with one. "The bastard!" she said. "The miserable bastard!"

Daniel replied, a tremor in his voice, "You've got it wrong, Annie. I'm the one who is a bastard."

"Oh Daniel! I'm sorry! I…"

"Don't worry." He dropped a kiss on the top of her head.

They lay still, Anne thinking hard. She asked, "Do you know where this earl lived?"

"Everyone in the village knew where the Earl of Preston lived. He lived at Preston Abbey, which is about twenty miles from our village. He has a famous stud there—he raises racehorses. Needless to say, he never comes near our village, which is probably why my mother thought she'd be safe."

His voice was different as he said the words "my mother."

"Yes," Anne agreed softly.

He said flatly, "She had an affair with the earl, and when she discovered she was with child, he threw her out."

Anne disagreed. "That is not how Mr. Dereham described it to me. He said your mother told him that one of the earl's guests raped her after a drunken party at the Abbey."

At those words Daniel pulled his arm out from beneath her and jumped out of bed. Naked, lean, graceful as a cat, he stalked between the door and the window radiating a combination of violence and energy.

Anne sat up and pushed her hair away from her face. "Daniel? What are you thinking?"

He stopped for a moment to look at her. "It was the earl who raped her. It was no drunken guest, it was the earl."

"Yes," Anne said softly. "So it seems."

"I'll kill him. I'll kill the son of a bitch for what he did to my mother." His voice vibrated with fury.

Fear stirred in Anne's stomach. "Daniel," she said, her voice as calm and composed as she could make it. "Perhaps you ought to talk to your mother before you do anything."

111

At first, she didn't think he'd heard her, but then he stopped pacing and spun to face her. "Talk to my mother?" he echoed, as if she had spoken in a foreign language.

"Yes." A ray of moonlight was coming through the open window and Daniel had stopped in its light. It illuminated his dark head and sculptured body, but his eyes were shadowed. Anne wanted to go to him, to take him in her arms and comfort him, but she understood she couldn't do that. He didn't want that from her now. Her part was to be level-headed and reasonable.

She said, "Your mother had a good reason for keeping your father's name quiet. Clearly he had no intention of acknowledging you, and if he knew you were living so close he might have tried to harm you. She did her best for you, Daniel, and her best was very good. She married a fine man, who knew she was with child and who loved her enough to marry her anyway. And he loved you enough to be your father from the day you were born."

"Christ!" Daniel said in a shaking voice. "I can't see her now, Annie! What would I say to her? What could I say? It's been too many years...." He stopped, drew a deep breath, and repeated in a shaking voice, "I can't!"

Anne slid out of bed and went over to him. "It can rest for a while, my love. You'll know when the time is right. You'll fix it when you're ready to."

He looked down at her, this dark demi-god of a man she had married, and put his hand on her neck under her unbound hair. "Annie," he whispered and slid an arm around her. She shivered, then, leaning her body against his, she turned into him, reaching her arms around his waist.

"Let's go back to bed," he whispered.

And she whispered back, "Yes."

*

Anne slept later than usual and when she awoke the following morning she was the only one in the bed. She looked at the deep crease left from where Daniel had slept, and smiled. Then she dressed and went downstairs to breakfast. The silver covers were on the buffet and Jeremy came in to see if there was anything else she wanted.

"Mr. Dereham has breakfasted already, I gather."

"Yes, my lady. He was up quite early. He asked for the mail from yesterday, as he hadn't seen it. After he read it he asked me to pack a bag for him as he had to go to London for a while."

Anne was flummoxed, and must have looked it, as Jeremy said hurriedly, "He left a letter for you, my lady. It's on the table at your usual place."

Anne looked at her usual place and there it was, a white envelope. "I see. Thank you, Jeremy. I'll just have tea this morning."

"Yes, my lady."

He poured tea from the silver urn on the buffet and put in before her. "Is there anything else I can do for you, my lady?"

"No, thank you, Jeremy. You may go."

As soon as the door closed behind Jeremy, Anne opened the envelope and unfolded the crisp paper that was inside. She read:

> Dear Anne,
>
> I am sorry to go away in such a hurry, but I received a letter from my bank and there are several matters that need my immediate attention. You were sleeping so peacefully that I didn't want to wake you. I'm not certain how long it will take to straighten out this matter, but I will apprise you of my return as soon as I am able.
>
> Your husband,
> Daniel Dereham

Anne was stunned. After what had happened between them last night, that he should just turn his back on her and go off to London! Without even saying goodbye!

A swell of righteous anger surged through Anne as she tore the letter into four pieces. Damn him. Damn him damn him damn him. If he thinks he can get away with treating me like that, he has a surprise coming his way. From now on he can sleep in his bloody dressing room!

Then Anne, who had just thought more swear words than she had ever used in her entire life, swept up to her bedroom and cried.

PART TWO
FATHER AND SON

CHAPTER SEVENTEEN

Daniel did go to see his banker when he reached London, but that was not the real motive for his sudden retreat from Grex. He had awoken early the morning he departed, and, lying on his back, arm thrown over his forehead, he had thought about last night's encounter. After awhile he turned on his side to look at Anne while she slept.

She was so exquisitely lovely, with her long slender neck, ivory skin and silky dark hair. Her clear brown eyes were closed and her long dark eyelashes lay quietly against her faintly flushed cheeks.

The realization of what his inner self had known for some time rose to the surface of his mind. He loved her. He loved her and the thought terrified him. He had set out to make her love him, and he had been successful. But it had never been his intention to reciprocate that love. It was dangerous to love another person. This was one conclusion Daniel had drawn from his parents' deception, and he had sworn never to let himself be so vulnerable again. His marriage had been based on the solid sensible grounds of property and money, not love.

He hadn't wanted her to know about his birth, yet he had poured his heart out to her last night. She had already heard it from his father, of course, so he hadn't told her anything she didn't already know. She hadn't changed to him last night, but he knew very well the power of his seductive art. Today, in the clear cold light of morning, how would she feel to find she was married to the despised trash of some great noble?

The Earl of Preston hated him, and he already had enemies enough. The Manchester mill owners hated his factory, hated the way he was spending money on his workers, money they believed should go to the owner in profits. They were afraid Daniel's generosity might foment a revolution among their own workers, who would want what Daniel's workers had. The entire social situation in England was ready to boil over, and all the government could do was try to oppress the underclass even more. If anything happened to him, he had to make certain Anne would be provided for.

He had reached this point in his thoughts when Anne stirred. Daniel stopped breathing and watched as her eyelashes fluttered. Don't wake up, Annie, he thought. Not now. Don't wake up.

She turned onto her side and went back to sleep. He watched her, watched how her dark hair parted to reveal the tender white nape of her neck.

What the hell had he been thinking when he told her she could take charge of building a school? The school was one more thing the other mill owners would hold against him. Anne was his hostage to fortune. Should anything happen to her...it didn't bear thinking about. He'd find someone else who could take over the school. She wouldn't like that, but his concern wasn't to do what she liked, but what would keep her safe.

He rose quietly from the bed and went into his dressing room to change. The trip to London he had been putting off had suddenly become urgent. He wanted to hire security guards for the factory, and he needed to put some space between himself and his wife. She had got too close to him. It wasn't safe. Daniel had a light breakfast and in less than an hour was on his way to London.

*

The first thing Daniel did after he checked into the Pulteney Hotel was to pay a visit to Rundell and Bridge, one of the most well-known jewelers in London. He had brought a huge collection of jewelry home from India, dumped it in a bank box and forgot about it. It was time, he thought, to make certain his estate was in order. First on the list of things to do was to find out how much all that jewelry was worth.

Mr. Aubrey Spencer was the jeweler who accompanied Daniel to the bank. He was a man in his fifties, with narrow shoulders and a narrow face. His long thin nose was the most noticeable feature on his face, but Daniel found both shrewdness and intelligence in his gray gaze. He escorted Mr. Spencer to the bank in a cab.

The bank was ready for them. A secure room had been made available, with plenty of table space for the jewels. Once Daniel and Mr. Spencer were in place, the bank president himself brought in the two boxes. "Take as much time as you wish, gentlemen," he said before he left the room, closing the door firmly behind him.

Mr. Spencer began to remove the jewelry from the first box. After he had taken out four pieces and laid them on the black velvet cloth he had brought, he turned to Daniel, saying in a hushed voice, "Do you realize how rare and valuable these pieces are?"

Daniel wasn't surprised. "You should see the jewels Maharajah Pranav has in his possession. Indians collect jewels, and they pass them down from one generation to the next. In ancient times, they used jewels instead of money to trade or purchase the items they needed. Indians love beauty, you see, and to them nothing is more beautiful than the color, the design, the perfection of form that is a perfect stone in a perfect setting."

"And this Maharajah just gave you these jewels?"

"I did not steal them, Mr. Spencer," Daniel said evenly.

"Of c-c-course not...I d-d-didn't mean," the jeweler began to reply.

Daniel interrupted him. In the same even voice as before, he said, "These jewels were a gift to me from a man I greatly admired. They signify how highly he regarded me. I was deeply honored by that regard, but I do not possess the Indian passion for jewelry. Except for a few pieces I would like to give my wife, to me these gems represent what they represented to the early Indian traders. Money."

"Yes, I see." Mr. Spencer sounded suitably chastened. He turned his eyes to the four pieces laid out upon the black velvet cloth and picked up the pink diamond ring. He looked at the diamond through his lens, put the lens down and turned to Daniel. "This is a perfect pink diamond. Four carats I would say. Do you know how rare this is, Mr. Dereham? It is worth a small fortune all by itself. It's hard to believe anyone would part with it."

"He was quite fond of me and he had others."

"Others? Like this?"

"Yes."

"Dear God."

Next Mr. Spencer lifted an emerald necklace and looked at it through his glass. Holding it, he turned to Daniel. "There are sixteen emeralds on this necklace, Mr. Dereham, and countless number of diamonds."

Daniel had a sinking feeling he was going to be in this little room for a long time.

Much later, when Mr. Spencer had examined all of the jewels and was carefully replacing them in their wrappings to put back into the boxes, Daniel asked if the jeweler could give him an estimate of what the jewels were worth.

After making a point of excepting the pink diamond, which was basically priceless, the jeweler named a figure.

Daniel was stunned. He had expected to hear a large figure, but not one as large as that.

"If you wish to sell any of these immediately," Mr. Spenser said, "please let me know. Our firm will give you a good price, and you will avoid the nuisance of trying to sell them yourself."

"I thought I might sell a few pieces," Daniel replied. "I could use an infusion of cash about now."

"Then, please, come to see us. Or we will come to you!"

"Don't get your hopes up too high, Spencer. I plan to hold onto most of this jewelry. The only reason I wanted it priced now was that I am making my will and I want to split the jewels—half to my wife and half to my mother. That's why I wanted the valuation, so that they could be split fairly."

"I will be happy to give you a separate estimated price on each of the jewels, Mr. Dereham."

"Thank you," Daniel said sincerely. "That will be very helpful."

The jeweler left and the bank representative came into the room to collect the jewelry to return it to its safe.

"Is that all, Mr. Dereham?" the bank officer inquired.

Daniel had already slipped into his pocket a six-strand string of perfect pearls he thought would look lovely on Anne's long graceful neck. "Yes," he said. "That is all for now."

*

The following day Daniel ordered a carriage. If Anne wished to go anywhere he didn't want her having to travel in a hired chaise. She would travel the way all the fine ladies of the aristocracy traveled—in a carriage of her own. Carriages were safer than curricles, where you sat out in the open. An enclosed carriage would give her more protection.

The next stop Daniel made was to his solicitor to have his will drawn up. As he had told Mr. Spencer, all of the jewelry of which he was possessed was to be divided between his wife and his mother, "Mrs. Maria Owen of Redgate Farm, Candleford, Devonshire." Grex, the house, the property, the horses and all other appurtenances, he left to Anne.

He had spent some time debating what to do about the factory. He didn't want to leave it to Anne because it might be dangerous. But he wanted her to have some of the money the factory would generate. In the end he left the factory to "my dear friend and colleague, Robert Denver," with the stipulation that "one quarter of its yearly profit should go to my wife, Anne Elizabeth Sophia Dereham."

If all went well, and he survived long enough to have children, he could make the appropriate alterations.

He also hired a few ex-soldiers to act as security guards at the factory, and lastly, he visited an employment agency to ask them to try to find someone fitting to start up his school.

When all of this business had been accomplished, and he had no other excuses to stay away from Grex, he made plans to return home.

CHAPTER EIGHTEEN

The Jockey Club was having its quarterly meeting at its headquarters in Newmarket, the hallowed center of English thoroughbred racing. Eight men served as stewards, one of whom was the Earl of Preston.

After the business of the meeting had concluded, the members adjourned to a cozy room with old leather furniture and a well-stocked liquor cabinet. The room was redolent of horses and dogs, a familiar and pleasant smell for the members. Glasses were produced and wine and/or brandy were poured. The men made themselves comfortable and began to gossip.

"Did you hear about what happened to Merton?" Mr. Cruick asked. He was older than the rest of them and had been a mainstay of the Jockey Club for eons.

Two people had heard the story and four had not, so the tale had to be told. "Perhaps that will teach him to stay away from lightskirts who don't know their place," the old man concluded to general chuckles.

Sir Charles Bunbury, the Head Steward, turned to Lord Preston and said, "I say, Preston, I was speaking recently to a friend who has just returned from India. Did you know that bye-blow of yours was the darling of the Maharaja of Nawanger? Apparently, he started out working in the stable and ended up so close to the Maharaja that his eldest son was jealous and tried to have him killed. That's why he came back to England, you know. Didn't want to fall foul of the heir. Apparently, the Maharaja was so besotted he gave him a fortune in jewels to take with him."

Lord Simon Lowry said, "That's the fellow who married Grex's girl, right?"

"That's right," Sir Charles replied. "I heard he gave Grex an inordinate amount of money for the place, as well as taking the girl off his hands."

Sir John Barlow said, "This Dereham fellow came home spouting all kinds of reactionary ideas about 'social reform' and 'working communities.' I hear he's building a factory near Manchester with new cottages for the workers—even a school for the children! And the men only work eight hours a day! That kind of thinking can be dangerous, you know. Can't have the lower classes getting above themselves."

Sir Charles said, "If the man wants to invest his own money in a scheme like that, then I say let him do it. It can't hurt us."

A few of the other men were adding their opinions when the Earl of Preston exploded, "That upstart is not my son! I will call any man out who says he is! No one of Montford blood would ever behave the way he has!"

The other seven men stared at the earl in surprise. His face was the color of puce, the veins in his neck were distended and his narrowed blue eyes were daggers.

"No need to get so touchy about it, Preston," Sir John said. "Everyone says he's your son. The eyes—a dead giveaway you know."

"I will not have my name and my blood associated with that...revolutionary!"

The last word was said with such anger and disgust that old Mr. Criuck flinched.

The other seven men stared at their colleague, shocked at such a show of anger. A bastard son or daughter was nothing out of the ordinary among the English upper classes. It was certainly nothing to get upset about.

The earl stood up and warned, "I never want to hear that name spoken in this company again!" He picked up his hat and stalked out of the room; the seven remaining men watched in silence.

"Really," Lord Beaufort said when Preston had slammed the door behind him. "Everyone who has encountered Daniel Dereham has seen the resemblance. The eyes, the eyebrows, the coloring, are identical."

"I was afraid he'd have an apoplexy," Sir Charles said.

There was a short silence, then Lord Simon Lowry changed the subject. "What do you think of Eigar's chances in the fourth race tomorrow?"

The conversation shifted as the men refilled their glasses.

*

The wealthy men who owned mills near Manchester were members of a new class that was busily gathering riches and power into its hands, and they were not pleased with Daniel Dereham. They didn't like the spacious new factory, they didn't like the village built especially for the workers, they didn't like the ban on women and children working, and they really didn't like the eight-hour day.

"He's coddling them, is what he's doing," Geoffrey Margat, the owner of one of the oldest cotton mills in Manchester, said angrily. "I can hear my men talking about their 'rights,' and I tell you I don't like it. Look at those damn 'blanketeers.' They had the gall to try to march on London to protest to the King!"

Three of the most important mill owners in Manchester had gathered at Margat's house to discuss the "Dereham problem." The second most important man in the room spoke next. "They're het up already about the taxes on tea, sugar, beer, candles, paper, etc., etc." Alfred Grimsly was very disturbed. "With that Hunt fellow traveling around the country stirring up the mob, God knows what thoughts our men might be harboring."

"We could have a revolution like the Frenchies if we're not careful," Henry Brook declared. "Sidmouth has suspended the Habeas Corpus Act, so anyone under suspicion can be thrown into jail and kept there. Is there any hope Dereham might be vulnerable?"

"No chance," Margat said gloomily. "On the surface, he's doing nothing to stir up trouble. In fact, quite a few people think he's doing something good. No, the only way he'll be stopped is if we do it ourselves."

The three men looked at each other and nodded in slow agreement.

"But how?" Brook asked practically.

"Now that is what we are here to discuss," Geoffrey Margat said.

CHAPTER NINETEEN

Matthew Montford, Viscount Longford, only son and heir of the Earl of Preston, was sitting in the drawing room of his sister, Louisa, Countess of Westport, having tea.

"What did Papa do when he heard your name was going to be on the map as well as Smith's?" the Countess asked.

Matthew raised one black eyebrow. "What do you think he did?"

"Exploded?"

"You have it in a nutshell. He was so angry I thought he might have a seizure."

"We're not that lucky," Louisa said.

Matthew exhaled, but didn't contradict her. He took a pastry from the tray on the table in front of him and bit into it. "I'm starving," he said.

"I can send for something more sustaining than cream cakes if you like," his sister said.

"I can wait until dinner."

Matthew always stayed with his sister when he came to London. One never knew when his father might descend on the family townhouse, and Matthew and Louisa avoided their father like the plague. Their other two sisters, Joanna and Margaret, did not keep London townhouses, but spent most of their time at their husbands' homes in the country. Matthew was the third child of the Earl of Preston and Louisa the fourth. They were a year apart and had always been close.

"I thought he might become less tyrannical now that you have produced a son."

"Well, he hasn't. I have done my duty, Louisa. I married a girl Papa approved of, and together we have produced a son. It's time that I pleased myself, and this project of Smiths is what I want to work on."

"You and your rocks," his sister said affectionately. Matthew had been studying geology ever since Oxford and she knew how passionately he loved being out in the field.

He grinned. "I know."

Matthew was a nice-looking man of twenty-four. He had the blue eyes and black hair of his family, but his features were less harsh than his father's. Lord Preston thought his son was effete because he wasn't a bruising rider to hounds and a member of the Four-In-Hand Club. The Earl could not forgive his only son for preferring rocks to horses. When Matthew was young his father's contempt had been painful. As an adult, he had learned to ignore it.

He took a sip of his tea and looked around the drawing room. "Have you been decorating again, Louisa?"

She smiled. Louisa was an attractive woman, also with black hair and blue eyes. She had made a good marriage and produced a son and daughter for her older husband, who adored her. "I just had the walls repainted and new draperies made. The room was too dark; I never liked it."

"Well, it looks very pretty now."

Louisa looked pleased. "Thank you, Matthew. Robert likes it too."

Matthew grinned. "Robert would like it if you painted it black."

She smiled again.

"On another subject," Matthew said, "have you ever seen this mysterious half-brother of ours whose very existence is driving our father mad?"

Louisa sipped her tea, then answered, "I saw him at a few balls last season, before he married the Grex girl."

"Ah yes. The Grex girl. That is another thing that is driving our dear Papa insane. He deepened his voice and made it more staccato as he imitated his father. It sickens me to think a bastard factory owner has made himself Master of Grex. Grex—one of the most ancient families in England! It even goes back further than we do. And now the son of a housemaid is master there? It's a disgrace, I

128

say. Grex has a lot to answer for, selling his birthright like that. Shame on him, I say. Shame on him!"

Louisa had begun to giggle after her brother's first sentence. "You do him very well, Matthew. It never seems to occur to Papa that he created this monster he hates so much. After all, it was he who impregnated a housemaid and made her a mother."

"Dereham wouldn't concern him if he hadn't turned himself into such an important man. If he had stayed with his mother the maid, and stayed out of sight, the thought of his existence wouldn't bother Papa at all. But the man has made himself famous; first by acquiring a huge fortune, something that is always of interest to the *ton*, and second by building an extraordinary sort of cotton mill."

"Extraordinary?" his sister said. "What's extraordinary about a cotton mill—except for the fact that it's trade?"

"Moresack was telling me just yesterday that Dereham is some kind of philanthropist. He's built cottages for all his workers and—most amazing of all—they only work eight hours a day."

Louisa's blue eyes stretched wide. "That is amazing. How can he make a profit if his people only work part time?"

"That is what everyone is waiting to see."

Louisa changed tack. "He's stunningly good looking."

"Is he?" Matthew grinned. "Does he look like me?"

"He has black hair like you, and the same eyes, but he has the face of an angel. Not like you."

Matthew managed to look insulted. "Thank you very much."

"You're welcome," his sister replied pleasantly.

Matthew continued with his inquisition. "You never spoke to him?"

"No."

"I heard that he's in town right now. I think I might call on him."

"Matthew. If Papa finds out you've called on Daniel Dereham he won't just explode, he'll...erupt. Like a volcano."

"I'll keep it quiet Louisa. But I can't help but think that this man is my brother. I've never had a brother, only sisters. I'd like to meet him."

Louisa looked around her drawing room, as if she suspected someone might be eavesdropping. She lowered her voice. "If you do, you must tell me all about it."

"I will," he said.

*

Daniel had been making the rounds of employment agencies looking for someone to take charge of creating a school for him. He had interviewed a number of women, but none of them impressed him. Were all schoolteachers so short of sparkle and ideas?

He had just about decided to see if he would have better luck in Manchester than in London, when one of the hotel's immaculately dressed staff knocked on his door and presented him with a card. Daniel looked at the name—Matthew Montfort, Viscount Longford. A note was scribbled on the back, "May I come up?"

Daniel was not familiar with the name, but he wasn't averse to seeing what the man wanted. "Bring him up, please," he said to the hotel footman.

Daniel was clearing some papers off the tea table of his sitting room when there was a light knock. "Come in," Daniel called. The door opened and a young man appeared. "Lord Longford," Daniel said amiably, as he went toward the door, "what can I do for you?"

He held out his hand, looking politely into the other man's face. Their eyes met and Daniel froze. His hand was taken into a firm, warm grip, and Lord Longford said, "I decided it was time that I met my brother."

Daniel was ashen and only just managed to say, "Sit down, please. May I offer you something to drink?"

"Don't bother." Matthew made his way to the sofa and sat behind the paper-strewn tea table.

Daniel slowly followed him and sat in a wing chair placed at right angles to the sofa. "To what do I owe the honor of this visit?" he asked, his voice carefully neutral.

"As I said, I wanted to meet you." Matthew regarded his half-brother with interest. "I can see what Louisa meant when she said you were 'stunningly good looking.' You got your coloring from our side of the family, but your mother must have been a beauty."

Daniel said, "Let's leave my mother out of this conversation."

"All right," Matthew said pleasantly. "Our connection is through my father, after all."

"I want nothing to do with your father," Daniel said. There was a white line around his mouth.

"Frankly, neither do I," Matthew replied. "He's always been a tyrant, and it's got worse as he's got older. I'm only up in town to escape his company down at Preston."

When Matthew had finished, Daniel asked cautiously, "Why have you come to see me?"

"I was curious," Matthew answered frankly. "I wanted to see the man who had thrown my father into such paroxysms of hatred. He really is irrationally furious about your existence, you know. Hard to figure out why, when, as my sister pointed out a few hours ago, he was the one responsible for your existence. Have you ever met him?"

To his own surprise, Daniel found himself telling Matthew the story of his encounter with Lord Preston at the racetrack when he was sixteen.

"I see he was his usual charming self," Matthew declared. "You were fortunate you didn't grow up with him. He treated his dogs better than he did my sisters and me. To be frank, we all hated him. My two older sisters married the first year they were out in society, and my younger sister, Louisa did the same. I at least got away when I was at school, and then at Oxford. Unfortunately, since I'm his heir, I have to see more of him than they do."

Daniel was starting to feel curious. "What about your mother?"

"She was petrified of him, poor thing. She died having Louisa and I think it was a merciful release." He smiled at Daniel. "You had the best luck of all, old chap. You got to go out to India, which I would love to see, and I hear you came back with a fortune in jewels."

"The maharajah was very generous," Daniel said stiffly.

"I've been hearing you have very advanced ideas about working people," Matthew said. "The eight-hour day and all. Do you actually employ your men for only eight hours a day? How can you make money that way?"

Crystal blue eyes looked into crystal blue eyes. "If you're just being polite, I would rather you left," Daniel said.

Matthew sat up. "I hope I am always polite, but I am not here simply to take up your time. I'm interested in your ideas and would like to hear them from your own lips."

There was a silence as the two men studied each other. Then Daniel's face relaxed. "Very well." He leaned back in his chair and began to explain. At the end of an hour's worth of question and answer, the two men were much in charity with each other.

"If you're ever looking for a partner, please call on me," Matthew said. "My mother left me pretty warm in the pocket and I would very much like to invest in your factory project."

"Thank you, my lord," Daniel said.

"Please, call me Matthew. We are brothers after all."

Daniel looked a little alarmed. "Do you plan to acknowledge me as such?"

"Would you like that?"

"No!"

Matthew looked hurt, and Daniel hurriedly added, "It's not that I don't like you, Matthew. I do. But I am not interested in being a member of a society I heartily dislike. When I was a child my mother used to read me the tales of Robin Hood. He became my hero. Well, the people in society seem to me the opposite of Robin

132

Hood. They don't take from the rich and give to the poor; they take from the poor and give to themselves."

Matthew got to his feet. "You're a good man, Daniel Dereham, and I'm proud to have you for a brother. You just carry on with what you're doing and the world will be a better place."

Daniel smiled. Matthew looked at him and said soberly, "Don't ignore my father's hatred, Daniel. He just may do something drastic to remove you permanently from the scene. I say this in all seriousness. Watch your back."

"I always watch my back," Daniel returned calmly. "I learned that in India."

Matthew held out his hand. "I'm delighted to have found you, Brother."

"Thank you," Daniel returned formally.

The two men held their handshake for a few more beats than necessary, then their hands fell apart and Matthew took his leave."

Daniel stood for a while, staring at the closed door, then slowly turned back to the papers on his tea table.

CHAPTER TWENTY

After Daniel left, Anne tried to keep her anger with him at full blast. But after a week, however much she stoked its fire, her anger slowly ebbed and desolation crept in.

He didn't love her. He couldn't love her and have left her the way he did. He had confided in her, and made passionate love to her, and she had believed she had finally broken through that invisible barrier that seemed always to stand between them. And the very next morning he had taken himself off to London with only a terse note to tell her where he was going.

She had thought he loved her, and she had been wrong. Instead of bringing them closer, the sharing of his life story had widened the gap between them. He had regretted confiding in her so much that he had run away. There was no other way to interpret his sudden flight.

Anne was bitterly hurt, but she called on her pride to rise above it. She would be just as aloof as he was. There would be no more melting inside whenever he so much as looked at her. She was her own woman. She still had Grex, and now she had a project to throw her heart into. She and Bonny would make the best damn school in the entire country for those factory children. Daniel could do as he liked. She wouldn't care.

*

After a few weeks in residence at the Pulteney, Daniel had accomplished everything he planned to do in London. He had heard from Robbie that the security guards were safely in place at the factory, and he had attended to the legal disposition of his property should he die. The only thing that had been keeping him from an immediate return to Yorkshire was the new coach he had purchased, and the coach was now ready. Matthew had told him about some beautiful matched bays someone was selling to pay off gambling debts, and Daniel had an appointment to drive out to Kent to look at the horses that afternoon. If he purchased them, he could think of no more excuses to remain in the city.

135

It's not that he didn't want to return to Grex; he wanted desperately to be home again. He wanted just as desperately to see his wife, but another part of him shied away.

The truth about his illegitimate heritage had horrified Daniel so profoundly that he was afraid Anne would have the same reaction. He had never intended to tell her the truth, and then, like an idiot, he had blurted out the whole sordid story.

He had realized as soon as he awoke the following morning that it had been a horrendous mistake. Anne had known that in marrying him she was marrying beneath her class, but she hadn't known she was marrying a bastard—a child who was so unacceptable he'd been cast off by his own father like a piece of garbage.

The worst part was, he knew Anne would never say a negative word about his birth. She was far too kind to ever let him know how much she disliked the fact that the father of her children was an illegitimate cast-off. But he would know how she felt, and it would eat away at him. The marriage he had come to depend on as the rock upon which the rest of his life rested, would be destroyed.

*

The bays Matthew had recommended impressed Daniel, and he bought them from the heartsick baron who hated to see them go. The new coach was ready and Daniel hired a coachman who was recommended by Lord Neviss. Daniel would ride home on the front seat with this coachman to assure himself the man could indeed be trusted with his horses and his wife.

Two days before he planned to leave for Grex, Daniel was walking back to his hotel after meeting with a friend from India. It was growing dark and a thick fog had descended on London. As he inhaled the foul London air, he longed with all his heart to be back at Grex—back to its pure air, its rolling countryside, its paddocks filled with his precious horses. He wanted to go home so badly, but…he was afraid. He, who at sixteen had boldly set out for India with only a small sum of money in his pocket; he, who had ventured into an unknown country without a friend in the world;

he was being forced to admit he was afraid to go home and face his wife.

Daniel was brooding on this very thought as he walked through the increasing darkness and fog, when suddenly, out of the heavy mist, three men surrounded him. They were carrying heavy wood clubs and the first blow landed with excruciating pain on Daniel's left shoulder. Instinctively he ducked and the second blow missed his head by inches.

Daniel had been in brawls like this in the streets of Calcutta, and he knew how to fight dirty. Quickly and efficiently he disabled all three of his husky attackers, leaving them sprawled on the ground groaning in pain.

"Who sent you?" he demanded as his hard eyes moved from face to face in the dim light. His own breathing was even and his tone was imperative.

No one answered. Daniel removed a small revolver from where it had been tucked into the back of his trousers and pointed it at his would-be attackers. "Who was it?" he said again.

"Don't know," one of them offered. He was breathing heavily through a very bloody nose.

"You got paid to do this," Daniel said, looking inexorably from one to the other. "Tell me who paid you, or else...." He moved the revolver.

"It was Mr. Grissom!" one of the other men yelled. "He made a deal with somebody to do you. Don't know who the cove was who paid 'im."

Daniel had heard of Grissom. He was one of the two or three men who were behind most of the crime in the city. "Ah," he said. Then, "You will tell Mr. Grissom for me that he would be wise not to make any more deals concerning my safety." His voice lowered and became remarkably dangerous. "I will stop it myself if I have to, but it would be easier for Grissom if he did it himself. Do I make myself clear?"

"Yes sir," the three men mumbled.

"Do not follow me." Daniel turned his back on them and once more began to walk in the direction of his hotel. Before he was out of hearing range, he heard one of the men say, "Where in hell did a gentry cove learn to fight like that?"

As Daniel walked into the elegant room that served as the Pulteney's entrance hall, one of the hotel footmen came up to him with a message. "Lord Longford called, my lord. He is waiting in your apartment." The man looked directly into Daniel's eyes, studiously avoiding his disheveled and somewhat bloody clothing.

Damn, Daniel thought wearily. The only thing he wanted at the moment was a glass of brandy and a nice hot bath. As he went up the carpeted stairs, the adrenalin that had flooded his body began to ebb, and his left shoulder began to throb. It had been a hard hit.

He opened the door to his rooms, affixed a smile to his face, and walked into the parlor. Matthew was sitting on the sofa but he stood up as Daniel appeared and started toward him, hand held out. "I'm sorry to intrude on you," he began, then he too noticed Daniel's clothes. "Good God! What happened? Have you been drinking?"

"No." Daniel walked to the wing chair that was placed perpendicular to the sofa and sat down, careful to protect his shoulder. "But I could use a drink right now. Would you mind getting me a glass of brandy? It's over there, on the cabinet. Pour yourself one while you're there."

Matthew filled a glass almost to the top and brought it to Daniel. "Here you go, old boy. Drink it down."

Daniel drank half the glass then laid it on the table next to him. "I had a little run-in with three ruffians on my way back here. They attacked me before I saw them. I must be getting careless now I'm back in England. I would have seen or heard them in India."

"You were attacked? Were you alone?"

"I was."

Matthew frowned and shook his head. "Not a good idea, Daniel. Especially not in the fog and the dark. Did they get anything from you?"

"No." Daniel drank the second half of his brandy. "They weren't looking for just anyone, Matthew. They were looking for me."

Matthew lips tightened and he said sharply, "Are you certain about that?"

"Yes. They told me a chap named Grissom paid them to jump me."

"Christ!" Matthew exploded to his feet. After pacing the length of the room once, he turned to face his brother. "I'm sorry, Daniel. I never dreamed my father would go this far."

"Your father?" Daniel was nonplussed. "Do you think your father hired those men?" He shook his head as if to clear it. "They were after me because of the factory, Matthew. It wasn't your father."

"I think it might be." Matthew was very pale as he returned to his seat on the sofa.

"No," Daniel said. "That doesn't make sense. I know he despises me, but I'm simply a nuisance to him. There's no reason for him to arrange my death!"

"You don't understand," Matthew said. "He more than despises you, Daniel. He hates you. It's bizarre, I know, but your existence is driving him mad. If his friends didn't know about your connection to us, then you wouldn't matter. But the thought that his bastard son is the owner of a revolutionary factory—and all of London knows it—is making him insane."

Daniel was frowning. "But...why should he care what I do? He's never acknowledged my existence."

Matthew leaned forward, picked up his glass, and drank half of his brandy. He returned the glass to the table with a click, and looked at Daniel. The brandy had put a little color back in his face. "My father has this ridiculous obsession about the purity of the Montfort blood. Our family is very old, you see. My forebears fought in the crusades and at Crecy and Agincourt. In my father's eyes, Montforts rank far higher than the present King of England and his family. He was furious when you married Lady Anne Grex and became Grex's owner. The Grex family is even older than ours, you see, and my father hates the thought of you contaminating their ancient lineage."

Contaminating. Daniel had thought that very word about himself.

Matthew continued, "My father still lives in the middle ages, Daniel. I've tried to enlighten him, to no avail. And unfortunately, my sisters—with the exception of Louisa—tend to agree with him."

Daniel shifted in his chair and winced as his shoulder felt the movement.

"You're hurt!" Matthew said.

"They surprised me and one of them got a bash in on my shoulder. As I said, I've become too sanguine now I'm in England."

"Let me get you another brandy," Matthew said.

Daniel held out his glass.

Once the two of them were settled again, glasses in hand, Matthew said gloomily, "You can imagine what dear Papa thinks of my interest in geology."

Daniel's black eyebrows arched. "I imagine he doesn't like it."

Matthew drank some brandy. "Hates it, Daniel. Absolutely, utterly hates it. But I have fulfilled my duty to the dynasty by producing a son, and I am determined to join Smith's work in Somerset again. His findings have been amazing."

Daniel finished his brandy and said, "Most of the mill owners in Manchester hate me. I was thinking they were probably the ones who hired Grissom."

Matthew looked up from his brandy glass. "Factory owners? Why should they want you out of the way?"

"Because they're stupid and short-sighted and terrified that my 'experiment' is turning their workers into revolutionaries."

"Daniel, listen to me. I cannot emphasize enough how much the government is afraid of all so-called revolutionaries. The Home Secretary, Sidmouth, is hysterical on the subject."

"What did the government expect when it suspended the Habeas Corpus Act?" Daniel leaned forward, ignoring the pain in his shoulder. "This government gave magistrates the power to send any person they deemed a danger to public order to prison! And these prisoners can be kept confined indefinitely. Sidmouth and his friends are making revolutionaries by such outrageous decrees."

"Daniel, my father thinks Sidmouth is wonderful. They both regard the lower classes as less important than cattle. Dear Papa is rabidly opposed to any change in the order of things. When he heard you were giving your employees an eight-hour day he almost had an apoplexy." Crystal blue eyes bored into crystal blue eyes. "Watch your back, Daniel. It wouldn't surprise me to learn my father had hired someone to get rid of you. I can assure you, it wouldn't bother his conscience in the slightest."

Daniel sat in silence, contemplating Matthew's words.

Matthew said, "When are you going home?"

"Thursday."

"Be careful, Daniel. I like having a brother and I don't want to lose you. And remember, if things turn ugly, it doesn't hurt to have a future earl on your side."

Daniel smiled. "Thank you, Matthew," he said sincerely.

He kept the smile pinned to his face until Matthew had closed the door behind him. Then he stood and, cradling his left arm with his right hand, he rang the bell to call for a bath.

CHAPTER TWENTY-ONE

Anne had received just two terse communications from her husband since he departed for London. The first arrived a week after his departure and advised her he was purchasing a carriage and four horses and would be bringing them home. He directed her to make certain Frankie had space for the coach as well as for the four new horses. The second communication reached Grex three weeks later. In it Daniel informed Anne he would be home shortly.

After the first note's arrival, Anne and Frankie had made certain that the space Daniel requested in the stables was provided. Then Anne had waited for what she expected to be her husband's imminent return with said horses and carriage.

The weeks went by with no sign of Daniel. During that time the days had grown shorter, colder and gloomier. At night Anne huddled in her solitary bed, trying not to think about how much warmer she would be if Daniel were beside her. For the first time since her marriage, Dorothy was allowed to join her mistress in bed. Daniel had evicted the little dog when they married, but Anne had no compunction about letting Dorothy sleep with her head on her absent husband's pillow. Dorothy could stay there permanently as far as she was concerned.

Daniel's second note had outraged all her sensibilities. The nerve of the man! she thought as she stared at the two lines of writing. He was treating her as if she were his housekeeper. Well he would soon find out he was mistaken. She lay awake for most of the night, counting over her grievances. She had to be strong, she told herself. He didn't deserve her love, and she most certainly would not offer it.

When Anne opened her eyes in the morning, and remembered Daniel would be returning to Grex that day, panic seized her. She drank a cup of tea in bed, hoping to settle her stomach, then slowly arose. She allowed her maid to dress her and took Dorothy down to the kitchen for her breakfast. Her brain wanted to get out on a horse, but her stomach was not cooperating.

She managed to eat a roll, then she took a tour of the house. She wanted Daniel to be stunned by the progress she had made in his absence. The servants' attic bedrooms were finished and furnished. The new rugs made the downstairs rooms look both elegant and cozy. And a carriage house was in the process of being constructed so Daniel would have a permanent place to house the coach and curricle, as well as the ancient trap Anne used to drive around the neighborhood.

Anne picked at her luncheon, then she and Miss Bonteen retired to the parlor. At two o'clock, after Anne had moved the figurines on the chimneypiece four different times, Miss Bonteen suggested she go upstairs and read. "You won't miss Mr. Dereham's arrival, my love," she said coaxingly. "You can see the driveway from your sitting room window."

Anne's nerves felt stretched as tightly as the string on a bow. "Perhaps I will," she said, and went upstairs. She picked up the book she had been reading and stared at the print without seeing it. After a few moments she got up and went to the window. She repeated this pattern eleven more times before she was rewarded by the sight of a splendid coach drawn by four magnificent horses coming up the driveway. She watched as the coach pulled up in front of the door and the man seated next to the driver jumped down from the high seat.

Her heart began to hammer. He wore a hat so she couldn't see his face, but only one man she knew moved that gracefully. It was Daniel.

She would have to go and greet him. As she turned to start across the floor to the closed doorway, a knock came and one of the new maids, Nancy, said, "Mr. Dereham has arrived, my lady."

"Thank you," Anne said. She passed out of the room and progressed down the stairs at a steady gait. He was still in the front hallway speaking to Miss Bonteen when Anne arrived.

"Welcome home," she said in a steady voice. "All of us at Grex are pleased to see you again."

He stepped forward to greet her. She looked up into that archangel's face and offered her hand instead of her cheek. His brows rose in surprise, but he took her hand into his, raised it to his lips and kissed it.

A treacherous shiver ran through Anne's body. She almost snatched her hand back. He smiled, but his eyes were grave. "I'm glad to be home," he said.

He looked thinner, Anne thought. He had been slim when he left, but he had definitely lost weight. Had he been eating properly? She said, "Have you eaten since breakfast? Would you like some tea?"

"I am rather hungry," he said. But the way he said it, and the look in his eyes as he regarded her, gave his words a meaning that made Anne flush. He smiled slightly, turned to Miss Bonteen, who had gradually taken on the role of housekeeper, and said, "Might we have it served in her ladyship's sitting room?"

"Of course, Mr. Dereham, Miss Bonteen replied. "I'll see to it right away."

"Shall we go upstairs?" Daniel said to Anne. "I have a few things I need to discuss with you."

"And I with you," she returned, relieved that her voice didn't tremble.

*

Daniel had known from the moment she spoke that Anne was angry with him. The coolness of her voice, the way she pulled her hand away after he kissed it, told him clearly she hadn't forgiven him for disappearing to London. As he went up the stairs behind her, he regarded her rigid back and thought about how he could bring her around.

The sitting room door was open and Anne went in. Daniel waited until she chose a single green velvet chair before he took a seat upon the room's rose-print sofa and said, "Anne, I'm sorry. I'm sorry I went off the way I did. It was stupid and thoughtless and hurtful, and I'm very, very sorry. Will you forgive me?"

145

"Of course," she said, clearly not meaning it.

He looked at her face, at the beautiful lines of her eyebrows, at the large long-lashed brown eyes that had always looked at him so honestly, at the long, swan-like neck that was so graceful. He loved her. How was he going to make this right?

"I had business in London that needed attending to," he said.

"So you said in your brief note."

This was not going well. "I should have waited to speak to you, I know. It was just…"

His voice trailed away.

"You didn't think it was important," she continued for him, her face pale and set.

"Of course it was important! But I had a dreadful head from drinking and I just wanted to get out into the air. I thought I could write you from London."

As soon as the words were out of his mouth he knew he had made a mistake. She picked up on it immediately. "But you didn't write me from London, at least not about your 'business.' You wrote me twice, once to tell me you had bought a carriage and once to tell me you would be arriving the following day. Was buying a coach the reason you went to London?"

"It was one of the reasons," he said cautiously.

She didn't reply but her whole expression told him she didn't believe him. He was beginning to get annoyed. Annoyed with himself for having been such an idiot, and annoyed with her because she wasn't forgiving him. There she sat, not three feet away, and he might have been on the other side of the ocean as far as she was concerned. He wanted her. He wanted to take her into his arms, to press his body against hers, to take her, have her, never let her go. He loved her. Couldn't she see that?

She said, "Are you going to tell me now what your business was?"

Damn. He had set a trap for himself. If he told her no, she would be even angrier. But he didn't want to tell her about the will. He still didn't want any questions about his mother.

She waited, and when he didn't speak, she said, "I see," in a tight little voice.

He saw the hurt she was trying to conceal and gave in. "I wanted to see exactly how much money the jewels I brought back from India were worth."

Her eyebrows lifted into two fine question marks, and he told her the sum that Rundell and Bridges had given him as an evaluation. Stunned, she stared at him wordlessly.

"Yes," he said. "It was more than I thought it would be."

She let out her breath. "That maharajah must have liked you very much indeed."

"There was plenty more in his palace and his storeroom. The rich in India are rich beyond the stretch of our English imaginations, Anne. Our aristocracy counts its wealth in land. The Indian princes count it in more tactile materials."

She was silent, waiting for him to continue. Doggedly, he went on. "I had my will drawn up. I know I should have done it when we married, but I never got around to it. If anything should happen to me, you and Grex will be well looked after, Anne. Half of those jewels will go to you."

The color drained from her face. She leaned forward in her chair, closer to him. "Are you ill, Daniel? Is that why you went to London?"

He heard the concern in her voice and was reassured. "I'm fine, Anne."

She sat back again. "I'm glad to hear it."

This time he leaned toward her, trying another apology. "Annie, I've said I'm sorry, and I am. I should never have left you the way I did. I won't ever do it again. Can't you forgive me? Can't we get back onto our old footing? We get along so well, sweetheart. Why create a rift between us?"

He neglected to say he had missed her. He neglected to say he loved her.

Anne stood up and smoothed down her skirt. She said in that cool voice he was coming to hate, "Of course I forgive you, Daniel, now that you have explained yourself so fully. But you are not the only one with news." She looked down at her hands, which were clasped across her stomach, then up again. "I am with child."

His eyes stretched wide. He jumped to his feet to go to her and hit his shin against the tea table. Cursing under his breath, he moved to stand in front of her. He took her hands in his and held them tightly. "You're having a baby?"

"Yes. I am having a baby. We are having a baby."

He blinked, trying to assimilate this news. He raised her hands to his lips and kissed them both. When she tried to pull them away, he wouldn't let her. "But that's wonderful, Annie! It's just...wonderful."

"I'm happy you are pleased."

He thought there was a softer note in her voice as she said these words, and held her hands even tighter. "I've been a fool," he said. "I ran away because I was afraid of what you would think of me now you knew I was a...a bastard. I felt I had lied to you by not telling you that before we married. I never intended to tell you, but then my...mother's husband...came and told you. And, well, I was scared what you would think."

Anne's brown eyes changed in a moment from ice to fire. "Daniel Dereham, are you seriously telling me you thought I'd reject you because of your birth? Don't you know anything about me? How could we have lived together for all these months and you not know I would never reject you? I love you! I don't care about your birth! I love you. I don't give a damn who your father was!"

Daniel's throat was tight and he felt tears dangerously close to his eyes. He hadn't cried since he was sixteen years old and he wasn't going to cry now. He reached out and pulled her against him. He was holding her too tightly but she didn't complain, only reached her arms around his waist and held him back. At last a shudder ran through his whole body and he loosened his hold.

"I'm hurting you," he said. "I never want to hurt you, Annie. God, I love you so much!"

She leaned back in his arms and looked up into his face. "Say that again."

"I love you," he said again. "I love you with all my heart and with every ounce of strength and energy that's in my body. You are the best thing that ever happened to me."

Her face was radiant as she raised herself on her toes and softly kissed his mouth. He smiled as she returned her heels to the ground. "How are you feeling? Have you been sick?"

"I'm fine," she said. "Just a little nauseated in the mornings."

"Only in the mornings?"

"Yes."

"That means you're feeling well just now?"

She reached up to cup his face in her hands. "I am feeling perfectly fine. Shall we go next door to our bedroom? Are you perhaps feeling a little weary from your long drive?"

He grinned and picked her up in his arms. "Come along and let me show you just how weary I am."

CHAPTER TWENTY-TWO

Anne fell asleep and when she awoke Daniel was gone. She reached out and felt the warmth on his side of the bed, just to make sure he had really been there. She had missed him so badly. She had ached for him. And he had come home. He had come home, and he had told her he loved her, and she believed him.

She lay, luxuriating in the cocooned warmth of the blanket, thinking about what he had confessed. Daniel was so self-contained, so sure of himself, so dismissive of class distinctions, that she had been stunned he could think his illegitimacy would change the way she felt about him. Her lips curved in a satisfied smile as she thought of how she had reassured him about that misapprehension.

Next, she remembered how he had held her tightly in his arms after their lovemaking and murmured into her hair, "I need you to be safe, Annie. If any strangers come to the door, tell Thornton not to let them in and send for me. Will you do that? I couldn't bear it if anything happened to you."

She had wanted to ask him what could possibly happen to her, but she could feel the tension in his body and in the arms that held her so close.

"Please," he said. "Will you do that for me?"

She hadn't asked him any questions, only replied softly, "Of course I will, Daniel."

The tension had drained out of his body. "Thank you, Annie. Thank you, my love."

She hadn't asked any questions because she thought she knew the reason for his concern. Anne had been reading the London papers that Daniel had delivered each day to Grex, and she was well aware of the turmoil disturbing the country. Millworkers were demanding more rights, and in response the government had passed the Six Acts, which restricted their rights even further. Orator Hunt had spoken in Manchester recently and had stirred a huge audience of millworkers to smoldering anger.

And, in all of this unrest, the Dereham Factory had been the shining star pointed to by all mill workers as what they wanted. There had been some angry harangues about Daniel in the local Manchester paper, citing him as a rich nabob who could afford to play the role of factory owner, something the everyday businessman could not afford to do.

She had seen the angry bruise on his shoulder. He had told her he slipped and fell. Daniel moved like a cat; he was not a man who slipped and fell. She thought of him making his will and her blood ran cold. He knew he was in danger. Her fingers closed so tightly around the bedclothes that they cramped. What could she do to keep him safe?

The answer came back, stark and pitiless; she could do nothing.

*

Ten days after Daniel arrived home, Anne was out in the front yard when she saw him coming down the walk leading Amit. There was a body draped across the stallion's back. She ran to meet them.

Daniel held up his hand as she approached. "Don't spook Amit any more than he is right now." The stallion was snorting out of dilated nostrils and tossing his head.

Anne slowed to a walk. "What happened? Who is that on Amit's back?"

"I don't know who he is. I'll tell you what happened as soon as I get him into the house. He's still alive. Can you send someone into town for the doctor?"

"Of course." Anne turned and made herself walk until she was at a distance from Amit, and then she ran. One of the footmen had seen her coming and was there to open the door.

"Richard, run to the stable and tell Frankie to go for the doctor! He can ride Bonfire." As the boy hesitated, looking toward Daniel, she said loudly, "Go!" and he bolted out the front door.

The butler came hurrying into the hallway. "Are you all right, Lady Anne?"

"I'm fine, Thornton, but Mr. Dereham is bringing home an injured man. Will you find Miss Bonteen and have her prepare a place to receive him? I don't want Mr. Dereham to have to carry him up the stairs."

"Of course, my lady."

By the time Daniel arrived at the door, Miss Bonteen had spread sheets on the sofa in the small room she and Anne sometimes used for their sewing. Anne was waiting for him, and she reached for Amit's reins so Daniel could lift the injured man off the stallion's back. As she took the reins, she saw blood on Daniel's sleeve and said sharply, "Are you hurt?"

At the alarm in her voice, Amit threw his head up in the air and began to back away. Anne didn't make the mistake of trying to hold the horse and moved with him. Daniel moved as well, keeping a supporting hand on the limp figure lying across the stallion's back. When Amit finally halted, Anne held him while Daniel lifted the unconscious man off the jittery stallion. Jeremy, who was a big strong lad, came out the door and said to Daniel, "Give him to me, sir. You had better see to the horse."

Daniel nodded, let Jeremy take the limp body, and turned to where Anne was trying to sooth a snorting Amit. Daniel took the reins from her, turned Amit and began to walk him toward the stable. He had reached the end of the walkway when Kumar appeared, running full out. When he reached them he said something in Hindu to Daniel, who responded in the same language and handed him Amit's reins. Kumar set off for the stable and Daniel came back up the walk to Anne. "The blood's not mine," he said.

"Thank God." Anne took a breath. "Frankie has gone for Doctor Seton. Who is this man? What happened to him?"

Daniel shook his head. "I don't know who he is, but I damn well want to find out. He tried to kill me."

*

Doctor Seton arrived and bandaged up the pistol wound Daniel had put in the stranger's shoulder. Then the doctor gave him a sedative so he could sleep. This annoyed Daniel, who wanted to interrogate the fellow, but the doctor assured him the patient would be far more coherent after a rest. Anne and Daniel retired to Anne's private sitting room upstairs. Daniel had a brandy and Anne a pot of tea.

"All right," she said, when Daniel closed the door behind them. "What happened?"

Daniel briefly contemplated making up a story, but when he looked into her worried eyes, he changed his mind. Anne was too smart to be fobbed off with a story. He stretched his legs out to the fire, which had just been lit, and said, "The fellow must have been watching me because he obviously knew where I rode when I took out Amit. We were galloping along, having a grand time, when I saw something ahead that caught my eye. It was just a glimmer on the path, but I pulled Amit up and we were trotting when we came up to it."

He took a swallow of brandy and Anne said tensely, "What was it, Daniel?"

He said, his voice grim, "Someone had strung a wire across the path, Annie. If we had galloped into that, Amit would have hit it and come down. I probably would have gone right over his head. If I hadn't been killed by the fall, it would be easy for someone to bash in my head to make it look as if I was."

Anne was staring at him in horror. "Was the man you just brought home the one who placed the wire?"

"I think so. I dismounted immediately, tied Amit and went into the woods to search. I knew he couldn't be far away. He would have had to stay around to make certain the trap worked."

Anne was looking so shocked that he took her hand into a comforting grasp, "I heard the sound of twigs breaking ahead and I got close enough to get a clear enough look at him to shoot. Then I brought him back here."

Anne's hand went rigid. "You were carrying a gun? You suspected something like this would happen?"

"I always carry a gun," Daniel said reassuringly. "It's a habit carried over from India."

Anne shook her head. "You expected someone would make an attempt on your life." She removed her hand from his. "You lied to me Daniel. You didn't get that bruise from a fall. You've been on the alert for something like this ever since you got home."

He sighed. "All right. I thought something might happen."

"What are you going to do about it? You can't just keep shooting people."

"I need to find out who is behind this mission to kill me so I can stop them."

"And this man might be able to tell you something?"

"I hope so—which is why we need to keep him alive."

There was a silence as they both thought about what had just been said. Then Anne asked, "Daniel, do you think these attacks might be connected to the factory?"

She had surprised him. "Why would you think that?" he asked.

"I've been reading the newspapers," she said. "I know about the unrest in Manchester. You aren't very popular with the mill owners there."

"I know, and I've suspected they might be after me. But the more I think about I, the less I believe it. They're businessmen, not assassins."

"If it's not the mill owners, then who could it be? What really happened in London to give you that bruise?"

He might as well tell her the whole truth, he thought. She deserved to know. And, if he was being honest, he wanted her to know. He wasn't alone any more, and it was a good feeling. He had Annie on his side. He said, "I was attacked on the street by a group of ruffians. I managed to overcome them and got them to tell me they had been hired by one of the biggest criminals in London." He raised an eyebrow. "In thinking about it, I realized that if the attacks were coming from Manchester, the mill owners would hire local cutthroats. They would know the locals, but I doubt they would know anything about the London underworld."

"But if it's not the mill owners, Daniel, who else could it be?"

"While I was in London Viscount Longford came to see me."

She gave him a bewildered look. "What does Viscount Longford have to do with any of this?"

"Do you know who Longford's father is?"

"No. Who is he?"

"The Earl of Preston."

Anne's lips formed a silent *O*.

He waited.

She said slowly, "That means Longford is your half-brother."

"Yes."

"And he came to see you?"

"Yes."

"Well...that was nice, wasn't it?"

"It was very nice. He's a nice fellow. I liked him. But, Annie, one of the reasons he came to see me was to warn me about his father—our father."

"The earl?"

"It seems the earl is furious that my name has become so prominent in reform circles. In fact, he hates me so much that Matthew thinks he might try to have me killed."

"But that's insane!"

"From what I've heard of the earl, he might well be insane. Matthew clearly thinks he is."

"But, Daniel...what are we going to do?"

That "we" resonated in his heart. "To begin with, as soon as this miserable sod upstairs wakes up, we're going to find out who hired him."

CHAPTER TWENTY-THREE

The doctor's sedative worked so well that the assailant didn't awaken until three in the morning. Daniel was sitting in his room when the man stirred, moaned, and asked where he was.

Daniel arose from his chair and went to stand over the bed. "You're at Grex, and I'm the man you were trying to kill," he said pleasantly.

The man in the bed looked to be in his forties, with a thin, weathered face, blue eyes and slightly hooked nose. He had a brown beard that was streaked with gray and there was gray in his brown hair as well. He looked up at Daniel and muttered, "Just my luck," in a deep Yorkshire voice.

"It was my luck that I saw your wire before my horse tripped over it," Daniel replied.

"What wire?" the man said.

Daniel raised an eyebrow. "The wire that is now in my possession. The wire that is going to hang you at your trial."

The man tried to sit up, gasped with pain and lay back again. "You shot me," he said, remembering.

"The doctor says you'll be fine."

The thin pale face on the pillow looked both frightened and bewildered. "Why would you call a doctor for me and put me in a bed in your house?" He tried to move and winced with pain. "What do you want from me?" he ended.

Daniel pulled his chair over to the bed and sat down. "You don't look to me like a man who'd take money to commit murder. You look more like a farmer," he said.

"I were a farmer once. Then them bloody enclosure laws took my farm away." He ran a tongue over his lips. "I'm thirsty. Any chance of a drink of water?"

Daniel poured a glass from the pitcher on the bedside table. He helped raise the man a little, and held the cup to his lips until the water was finished. Then he replaced the water glass and resumed his seat.

The man's strained blue eyes held Daniel's. "You're treating me right good for a man who tried to kill you. Why?"

"I want to know who hired you."

The man closed his eyes. "I canna be an informer. I have a wife and children…"

His voice ran down when Daniel laughed. "When I turn you over to the authorities you'll never see your wife and children again. Attempted murder is a hanging offense."

"Then God help me," the man said wearily.

"I will help you if you tell me who hired you."

His answer was a suspicious frown.

"I won't report your attempt on my life. And if your information leads to my finding out the truth about who is trying to kill me, I'll even give you a reward."

The suspicion still remained. "What kind of reward?"

"You're hardly in a position to bargain. Whatever reward I see fit to give you."

The man moved restlessly and let out a curse as he jarred his shoulder.

"What's your name?" Daniel asked.

"Michael Harmon."

"Well, Michael, are you going to cooperate with me or shall I summon the authorities?"

Michael's face had the look of a man who has been defeated too many times as he said gruffly, "It were Tim Williams. He lives in Leeds. He always has money, does Tim, and nobody knows how he gets it. I were working for Mr. Cassidy on his farm near Abberford when Tim come up to me and asked if I'd like to make twenty pound. He said he had heard my wife was sick and that I needed money. Twenty pound! Do you know what that would mean to Doris and me and the bairns? I've been slaving away on other men's farms for a pittance. Why twenty pound would change our lives, buy medicine for Doris..." He shifted again and looked up into Daniel's impassive face. "I didn't want to kill you, but it were..."

"I know. It was twenty pounds. So you took the job. Did Tim say why I had to be done away with?"

"I asked him, but he only said someone from Lunnon wanted it done and would pay me twenty pounds. Williams is from Lunnon himself, so I suppose he knows folk."

"Why didn't he do it himself?"

Michael shook his head. "Why should he take the chance when he knew he could find someone like me?"

Daniel stretched out his legs. "So the originator of this plot lives in London."

"That's what Tim said."

Daniel closed his eyes. It must be true then. Matthew had been right. His father was trying to kill him.

*

Anne was horrified when Daniel told her what Michael had revealed. "Your own father? Can such a thing be true, Daniel?"

He said, "I sat up for the rest of the night thinking about it. Remember—this man threw my mother out of his house the moment he heard she was with child. His child. He felt no sense of responsibility to her or to me. Matthew says he's furious because I'm associated with the push for social reform and everyone knows I'm his son. According to Matthew he thinks I'm degrading his ancient bloodline."

They were seated side by side on the chintz sofa in the morning room, and the sun was shining in through the windows. Anne's chest felt tight with the terror she was trying not to show. "How can we stop him? He's an earl, Daniel. If you accuse him no one will believe you!"

"I know," Daniel said.

Anne's hands were gripping each other so tightly her knuckles had turned white. She said, "You're certain Lord Preston hired this...this monster...to have you killed?"

"I'm as certain as it's possible to be. The men who attacked me in London gave me Grissom's name, and it makes sense. I know he pays a string of demobilized soldiers to carry out his so-called 'business' endeavors."

Anne fought to keep her voice steady. "What can we do? Lord Preston hates you, Daniel. And if you try to accuse him to the magistrates, they won't believe you."

"I know." His face looked bleak.

Anne slid closer and he put a warm arm around her. She said despairingly, "I can't even think of someone we could turn to. No one would listen to Papa or Percival."

They sat in silence for a few moments, then she straightened up, turned to him and said excitedly, "Perhaps we can hire someone to shoot this Mr. Grissom. Or better still, Lord Preston himself!"

"Good God." He turned to look at her. "Is this what I've brought you to—planning an assassination?"

She said fiercely, "I'd shoot him myself if I could get away with it."

He gathered her close again, dropping a kiss on her hair. "I appreciate the thought, sweetheart, but shooting isn't the answer. What we've got to do is get Preston to cancel his commission with Grissom. It's the only realistic way to solve this situation."

Anne was close to despair. Lord Preston had no conscience. He would never voluntarily give up his pursuit of Daniel. What were they going to do? What would she do if Daniel was killed?

It wasn't going to happen. She wouldn't let it happen. She said firmly, "You had better keep to the house until we come up with a solution. As we've just seen, you aren't even safe on your own property. That man upstairs is proof of it."

She felt his arm stiffen. "I'm not going to let that miserable excuse for a human being dictate where I go and what I do. I need to go on the attack, Annie, not hide in my house!"

Anne clutched the arm that held her. "Don't shoot him yourself, Daniel! Please don't shoot him. They'll hang you if you do!"

He loosened her fingers and looked down at her. "You're white as a sheet. I said shooting wasn't the answer, remember." His lips tightened. "I shouldn't have told you. It can't be good for you to be distressed."

His words stung and Anne glared at him. "Of course you should have told me. I'd be furious if you kept something like this to yourself. We're married...we're partners...we should face our problems together!"

He nodded, worry still showing in his eyes.

"I j-just don't want you to get killed," she said in a shaky voice.

"I have no intention of getting killed." He ran a gentle finger along her cheekbone. "Do you know, when I lived in India I was utterly fearless. I'd ride any horse, fight any man, climb any mountain, and damn the consequences. I never thought about dying." He pulled her closer again, resting his cheek on the top of her head. "But it's different now. I'm different. I have you, and soon I'll have a child. I know what it is to be afraid. I don't want to leave you. It's too soon."

Tears rolled down her cheeks and she buried her face in his shoulder to hide them.

"I think I might drive up to London to see my brother," he said. "He's the one who warned me against Preston. He knows his father's weaknesses better than I do. Perhaps he'll have a solution for us."

All of Anne's instincts screamed that London was dangerous. It was where that awful criminal lived. She said, "Couldn't you send your brother a note asking him to visit you at Grex?"

"No. I need to act quickly, before they hear this last attempt was a failure. I just hope Matthew is still in town." He bent his head to her and gave her a gentle, lingering kiss. "I know you're worried, but I will handle this. I have no intention of getting killed, or being put in prison. For the first time I can remember, my life has meaning, and I plan to hold onto it."

She forced a smile. "You had better." He moved as if to stand up and she put a hand on his arm to restrain him. "What am I supposed to do with that man upstairs?"

"Oh." Clearly, he had forgot all about Harmon. "I promised him a reward if his information led to my finding out who is trying to kill me."

"Daniel, that man tried to kill you. You can't give him a reward!"

"He's just some poor farmer whose wife and children are starving because he lost his farm and can't find work. Hold onto him until you hear from me. He won't be any danger to you, Annie. I'd never leave him here if I thought he was."

"How comforting," Anne said.

He grinned. "I'll write as soon as I know what is happening."

"Thank you."

"You're welcome," he said, and walked out into the hall. Anne heard him calling something to Thornton. He sounded happy.

She closed her eyes and began to pray.

CHAPTER TWENTY-FOUR

Daniel wasted no time but set off early the following morning for London. He took the curricle and froze, even with a heavy driving coat, scarf and leather gloves. After ten years in India, he felt the cold more than the resident English, and by the time he reached the Pulteney he was chilled to his very marrow. At the hotel he called for a hot bath and soaked for as long as the water remained warm. He got out reluctantly, dressed, and sat down to write a letter to his brother, hoping to God that Matthew was still in town.

By the time Matthew knocked on Daniel's sitting room door, it was close to dinnertime. "It took my sister's footman awhile to find me," Matthew apologized, as he came into the room and took off his leather gloves.

Daniel looked at his brother's perfectly fitted coat and pale pantaloons. "Aren't you freezing in those clothes?"

Matthew brushed off his concern. "It's not that cold and I had the coach. I thought you were in Yorkshire. Is something the matter? Your note sounded urgent."

"It is rather urgent, actually, and I need to discuss it with you. I hope I didn't take you away from something important."

"Not at all. What do you want to speak to me about, Daniel?"

A knock sounded and a hotel servant came in bearing a tray with a brandy bottle and two glasses. There was also a plate of beef sandwiches.

"I told them to bring something up when they saw you arrive," Daniel said, waving his brother to a seat. He poured brandy into a glass and handed it to Matthew. Then he poured one for himself and sat where he could see Matthew's face. Both men drank some brandy.

As he lowered his glass, Matthew said, "So what brought you back to London in such a hurry?"

Daniel said calmly, "Someone tried to kill me."

Matthew swore softly. "Tell me."

In the same calm voice, Daniel related the entire incident involving Michael Harmon.

Matthew went pale as he listened to Daniel's story. When Daniel had finished he asked, "And this Harmon was certain the order came from London?"

"That is what he said. My guess is that when Grissom learned I had returned home, he contacted someone he knows in Yorkshire. That would be this Tim Williams fellow. According to Harmon, Williams lives in Leeds now, but he's originally from London. Harmon says he always has money."

Matthew said in a hollow voice, "You think my father is behind this."

"You're the one who warned me about him," Daniel pointed out. "At first I thought the Manchester mill owners might have hired someone. But the more I thought about it, the less likely it seemed. The mill owners hate me enough to have me killed—I have no doubt about that—but I can't see them knowing about Grissom and how to contact him. If they wanted me dead they would have hired someone local. Manchester has its share of cutthroats who'd do just about anything for a few quid." He paused, then added, "And there's another thing. The mill owners would never have paid as much as twenty pounds."

A silence fell between them. Daniel sat quietly, watching his brother's down-looking face. He understood it was one thing to suspect one's father of murder, but quite another to have that suspicion confirmed. Daniel could only hope that Matthew wasn't going to walk away.

Finally, in an almost inaudible voice, Matthew said, "My father could easily have found out who to contact about a murder for hire. He sits on a Parliament committee that deals with crime in the city."

His face was white and drawn.

Daniel felt sorry for him and said sincerely, "I'm sorry to drag you into this sordid affair, Matthew, but I need your advice. Frankly, I don't know what to do. I can't denounce the earl; I have no proof. But I'm afraid he is going to continue this campaign until he succeeds and I am good and truly dead."

Matthew poured himself a full glass of brandy and took a healthy swallow. A little color returned to his face with the drink. He said in a more normal voice, "You don't have any ideas at all?"

"I did have one, but I promised my wife I wouldn't shoot him." Daniel too had poured himself more brandy and now he took a healthy swallow.

Matthew raised a single black eyebrow, a gesture so like Daniel's that it proclaimed their blood tie more clearly than a birth certificate. He said, "Your wife is right. Shooting him would only cause more trouble for you. What we need is to find something to threaten him with—other than reporting him to the authorities. I do not want to stand up in a court of law to testify against my father."

"I understand."

They sat in more silence, Matthew deep in thought, Daniel watching him and waiting. At last Matthew said slowly, "I think I may have an idea."

Daniel set his glass down on the table in front of him and leaned forward. "What is it?"

Identical blue eyes met and held. "My father breeds and races thoroughbred horses," Matthew said.

"Yes." Daniel couldn't see what this had to do with his problem, but he held his tongue.

"Let me re-phrase. He lives to breed and race thoroughbred horses. He despises me because I'm not the horseman he is." Matthew smiled wryly. "Ironically, you would have been the perfect son for him, Daniel. You're everything he wanted me to be."

Daniel said soberly, "Your father did me a huge favor by rejecting me. I ended up with a much better father than he ever could have been."

"I believe it," Matthew replied. He rolled his glass between his hands, looking at it intently. Daniel was quiet. Finally, Matthew said softly, "I think it might work."

Daniel leaned forward. "What's your idea?"

Matthew told him.

When he finished, the two men looked at each other, evaluating the other's reaction. Daniel said, "It might work, but first you'd have to get the cooperation of the Jockey Club. Do you know any of the stewards?"

"We don't need all of the stewards, all we need is Sir Charles Bunbury. None of the other stewards would question his authority. And my father is hardly the most popular man among them."

"Preston's a steward?" Daniel looked alarmed.

"He's a steward because his horses and stable are so successful that it became impossible not to vote him in." Matthew smiled wryly. "My papa has very few friends, Daniel. Dr. Johnson would call him an 'unclubbable man'."

Daniel, whose education had not included the work of the redoubtable Samuel Johnson, did not reply.

Matthew continued, "The racing season is over for the winter, but Sir Charles is a member of Brooks. I know because I've seen him there. Let me find out if he's in town. If he is, I'll talk to him straight away. If he's at his country house, we'll have to drive to wherever it might be."

He stood up and Daniel followed. "Thank you, Matthew," he said. "If I can ever do anything for you..."

Matthew lifted a hand. "We don't know if Bunbury will cooperate yet. I'll see if I can find him at Brooks and let you know what happens."

*

Fortune shone upon Matthew as he caught Sir Charles Bunbury donning his hat at Brooks' front door. When Matthew begged a few moments of private conversation, the baronet consulted his watch and decided he could spare fifteen minutes. He and Matthew repaired to one of the small, unoccupied sitting rooms on the first floor.

The Head Steward sat in one of the big comfortable wing chairs Brooks provided for its members and looked inquiringly at Matthew, who had taken the identical chair beside him.

"Thank you for your time," Matthew began. "This is not a conversation I enjoy having, but the situation is nothing short of dire."

The older man raised his bushy eyebrows but said nothing.

"It's about my father," Matthew began, and began to explain to Sir Charles the earl's vicious hatred of his bastard son.

"We've all heard him on the subject of Mr. Dereham," Sir Charles said when Matthew paused. "I agree he's quite irrational on the topic. But I don't see what I..."

"There's more," Matthew said grimly, and proceeded to inform the other man about the two attacks on Daniel's life and why he believed Lord Preston had instigated them.

Sir Charles was looking appalled. "But—are you certain about this, Longford? I'm sure the Manchester mill owners would like to see Dereham dead. They well might be the ones behind these attacks."

"We don't think they are," said Matthew, and he proceeded to detail the reasons why he and Daniel did not think it was the Manchester mill owners. He ended with the news that the earl sat on a committee responsible for investigating crime in London. "He had every opportunity to know how to contact one of London's major criminals. The Manchester mill owners, on the other hand, certainly did not."

Sir Charles thought for a long moment, during which time Matthew ceased to breathe, then the Chief Steward said explosively, "This can't go public! London has tens of thousands of half-starved unemployed men just looking for an excuse to riot. If those rabble rousers Hunt and Cobbett find out that an earl has commissioned the murder of a man who is known to be a friend of the mill workers, God knows what might happen!"

Matthew, who hadn't given any thought to the social implications of Daniel's situation, was quick to agree. "Just so, sir. The results could be cataclysmic."

Sir Charles stood and began pacing up and down the room. Finally he stopped before Matthew to say, "Dereham is his son for God's sake. What's the matter with the man?"

"Pride, Sir Charles. Overweening pride in his bloodline. It's become an obsession with him."

Sir Charles' gray eyes raked Matthew. "Why have you come to me about this, Longford? I carry no weight in the parliament. What do you expect I can do?"

Matthew spoke with urgency, "The only thing that can stop my father from this insane campaign is to threaten him with the loss of something he prizes more than anything else in the world. That is why I have come to you."

The bushy eyebrows lifted slowly as Sir Charles understood. "Ah. You want me to threaten him with losing his position as a steward of the Jockey Club? He would hate that, I agree, but I don't think it will..."

Matthew leaned forward, shaking his head. "No. What I want, Sir Charles, is for you to tell him that if anything happens to Daniel Dereham, he will be barred for life from racing his horses on English tracks."

Sir Charles let out a long breath. He sat down and turned to Matthew. "I'm sorry, but the Jockey Club hasn't the power to do such a thing, Longford."

Matthew's mouth set in a grim line. "Then tell him that if anything happens to Daniel, no gentleman will start his horse against him ever again. That is within your power I believe, and it would be just as effective."

Sir Charles' eyes narrowed. "No gentleman will start...mmmm..." He nodded slowly. "Very clever, Longford. Very clever. Yes, I think I might be able to do that."

"Would you need the support of the other stewards?

"Not if Preston agrees to stop the attacks against Dereham. If he does that, no one else need know. If he doesn't agree, then I will have to take it up with the other stewards."

"Do you think they would agree?" Matthew asked nervously.

"I doubt the issue will arise. Your father will not chance losing his ability to race in England."

"I didn't think he would."

"You know him well. He's a brilliant horseman. It's a shame he's such a repulsive human being."

Matthew sighed. "Yes, it is." He gathered himself and asked, "When will you speak to him?"

"I'll send a note that I wish to meet with him on a Jockey Club matter." Sir Charles stood once more. "I will inform you of the outcome, Longford. Where can I reach you?"

"A letter to the geological society will reach me, Sir Charles."

"Very well." Sir Charles smoothed his coat. "I must be off."

"Yes, sir. Thank you for meeting with me."

"Hmm," said Sir Charles and left the room, neglecting to shake Matthew's hand.

CHAPTER TWENTY-FIVE

Sir Charles was true to his word and as soon as he returned home he composed a letter to the Earl of Preston requesting a meeting with him at Jockey Club headquarters in Newmarket in three days' time. Since Sir Charles always had business to attend to in Newmarket, he repaired there the day before his appointed meeting with Preston, spent some time speaking with the track groundskeepers, had an excellent dinner with Lord Meryon at his Newmarket Stud, and went to bed. Early the following afternoon he was sitting in his office going over some studbooks when the Earl of Preston walked in.

It was a brief and deeply unpleasant meeting. The earl sat on the opposite side of Sir Charles' desk and said irritably, "What can be so urgent, Bunbury, that you must summon me in such an extraordinary manner?" The earl looked around the empty room. "And where are the other stewards?"

Sir Charles slowly closed the thick book then said, "This is not a matter that concerns the other stewards, Preston. This is a matter that concerns you alone."

The earl's iron gray brows rose in surprise. "I cannot conceive what you might be talking about."

Sir Charles sighed. He had not been looking forward to this interview. "Your son, Lord Longford, came to see me a few days ago," he began. "Apparently he has become friends with Daniel Dereham and…."

Sir Charles' words were cut off by the sound of Preston's hand slamming down on his side of the desk. "Damme! What did I ever do to deserve such a son? When he's not digging around in the dirt, he's making up to that scoundrel Dereham!"

The earl's face was alarmingly red. Sir Charles said mildly, "What have you got against Dereham? He seems to be a decent sort. He's interested in helping the mill…"

His words were cut off again, this time by Preston's shouted reply: "He parades himself around London, passing himself off as my son! He's not my son, he's a bastard! I made it clear to his mother that I wanted nothing to do with her or with her brat! And now my legitimate son, my heir, is cozying up to the scurrilous bastard. Well, I won't have it, I tell you. I won't have it, Bunbury! I won't have my blood associating with that...that piece of garbage!"

Sir Charles had listened to this tirade with an impassive face. If he had harbored any doubts about Lord Longford's accusation, they were put to rest by the look on Preston's face. He was so enraged that the veins on his neck were bulging. Sir Charles waited a moment, then said, "Longford told me that Mr. Dereham has been troubled by several attempts on his life."

"It's a shame that they failed!" Preston said forcefully. His face was the color of puce. "We can only hope the next attempt will be more successful!"

Murder was looking out of the Earl of Preston's blue eyes. Sir Charles said mildly, "Lord Longford is very concerned about his brother." As the earl began to object to the use of the word *brother*, Sir Charles held up his hand. "He is also concerned about you, Preston. He does not want his father to go to prison for conspiring to murder Daniel Dereham."

Some of the high color drained from the earl's face. "Longford said that? He actually came to you and said he believed I was trying to have Dereham murdered?"

"He did."

"That miserable, crawling piece of shite. He doesn't even like horses. He'd rather dig in the dirt. Can you believe that, Bunbury? A son of mine who doesn't like horses? I don't know why I'm surprised he cozied up to Dereham. They're two of a kind—a disgrace to the blood that runs in their veins."

"Are you admitting that you have tried to have Mr. Dereham murdered?" Sir Charles said.

The earl's head lifted, like a horse that smells danger. "I didn't say that."

"No, you didn't, and I am not going to try to get you to say it. What I am going to say, Lord Preston, is this. If anything should happen to Daniel Dereham, if he should in anyway be maimed or killed, I will make certain that no English gentleman will start his horse against you ever again."

Silence.

"You can't do that," Preston said finally.

"We did it once to the Prince Regent," Bunbury pointed out.

Color flooded back into the earl's face. "You wouldn't dare. You would never accuse me—a lord of the realm!—of murder. No one would believe you."

"The Jockey Club doesn't have to publicize a reason for what we do, we can simply do it on our own authority. And I have no doubt that the other stewards will follow my lead, Preston. You know they always do."

Preston shifted in his chair, then said in an agitated voice, "I am not trying to have Dereham killed! I don't like him, I've never made a secret of that, but I'm not trying to have him murdered."

"Then you will have to pray that the person who is responsible for the attacks is not successful."

The earl cursed, long and fluently.

"Do we have a bargain?" Sir Charles asked when Preston finally ran out of words.

The earl rose to his feet. In a tight, furious voice he said, "I am sure that in the future, Daniel Dereham will be quite safe. Good day to you, Sir Charles."

The earl stormed out of the room, his boots very loud on the unpolished wood floor.

*

While they were waiting to hear the results of Sir Charles' meeting, Matthew insisted that Daniel move out of the Pulteney and join him at his sister's house in Berkeley Square. Daniel had refused at first, but Matthew had been unrelenting. "Louisa and Westport aren't in town at this time of year, and there's only a skeleton staff on duty. You won't be putting anybody out, and I want you in a safe place until we hear from Bunbury."

Daniel had finally given in, more to placate this half-brother he had become fond of than to protect his own safety. The two young men spent their time playing cards for a guinea a hand. Daniel also learned a great deal about geology, which he found very interesting. For his part, Matthew learned a great deal about India and Daniel's life there, which caused him to regard his younger brother with a great deal of respect.

Finally, on the morning after Bunbury's meeting with the Earl of Preston, a messenger came to the door of 17 Berkeley Square with a missive from Sir Charles: Meeting successful. There will be no further attacks. Mr. Dereham is safe.

Finally Daniel was free to go home.

CHAPTER TWENTY-SIX

As soon as Daniel's curricle pulled up to the front of Grex, the footman Anne had watching for him told her of his arrival. She was standing on the front step when Daniel reached her, caught her up in his arms, and walked through the door into the hall with her. Once inside he set her down, but he didn't let her go. Anne, rejoicing in the strength of his arms around her, said breathlessly, "Thank God you are home! I've been so frightened Daniel. Oh, thank God you're home!"

Daniel said, "It's all right, my love. It's going to be all right. Preston has sworn to leave me alone."

She leaned back so she could see his face. "Are you sure?"

"Yes." He loosened his grip on her. "If you give me something hot to drink, I'll tell you about it. I'm freezing."

Daniel shed his outer layers of clothing and they went upstairs to Anne's sitting room, where a fire was burning briskly. She sat close to Daniel on the sofa, so she could feel the warmth from his body. She had spent the week terrified she was going to get news of his death, and needed the reassurance that he was still alive.

Over a pot of hot tea, he told her about his meeting with Matthew and about Matthew's plan. He told her how Sir Charles Bunbury had helped them. He assured her the Earl of Preston would no longer be a threat to them. He put an arm around her shoulders, kissed the top of her head, and told her he was safe.

When Daniel had finished, Anne tilted her head and touched her lips to his throat. "I love you so much," she whispered.

He said huskily, "Let's go to bed."

She smiled and let him pull her to her feet. In silence they walked together into the bedroom. Dorothy was comfortably ensconced on the bed, and Daniel briskly escorted the indignant little dog to the door. He locked it after her and said to Anne, "Let me help you with your dress."

After he had undressed her, she lay on the bed watching him disrobe. He was so perfect, she thought. Just watching him moved her to tears. He came to the side of the bed and bent to lay his lips on her stomach. "Our baby," he said, his voice full of wonder.

"Do you hope it's a boy?" she asked.

He lifted his head and looked at her. "I think I would like a daughter. A little girl as beautiful and kind and loving as her mother."

"Oh Daniel." Anne's voice choked with emotion.

He lay down next to her, kissing her breasts and throat until his lips reached her mouth. Anne kissed him back with all the passion she had in her, loving the feel of his strong back, the warmth of his skin, the feel of his hair as it slipped through her fingers like heavy silk. He's here, she thought. He's here with me and he's safe. I don't have to worry any more.

Then he slid over her and all thinking stopped. She opened to him as a flower opens to the sun, yielding her softness to his power with joyous abandon. Holding tightly to him, she gave herself up to the pleasure that washed through her as he took them both deep into the dark center of creation.

Afterward he lay against her, and she felt the heat radiating from his body, the heavy beating of his heart. "I love you," he said. He picked up her hand, held it against his cheek, and she felt the prickly roughness of his unshaven skin.

Thank you, God for giving me this man, she thought.

He said, in almost an echo of her own thought, "You have given me so much, Annie. A home, a baby, and most of all your love. I am a very lucky man."

After a long moment of peaceful quiet she said softly, "There is one question I have always wanted to ask you."

"Oh? What is it?" He was beginning to sound sleepy.

"Why did you want Grex so much, Daniel? Why didn't you just build your own new house instead of putting so much money into restoring an old one?"

"Ah..." He was silent for so long that she didn't think he was going to answer her. At last he said quietly, "I didn't want a new house. I wanted an old house. A house with history."

"Yes, but why?"

His voice was so low she had to strain to hear him. "It had to do with my real father. He despised me and I wanted to show him I was just as good as he was. That I had land, and an historic estate, just like he did. It was in my mind the whole time I was in India, that I would return home and show him."

Daniel turned his tousled head on the pillow and looked at her. "That's it, Annie. I know it sounds childish, but that's the real reason I bought Grex."

Her heart ached for the rejected boy he had been, but she blinked back tears and smiled. "I'm glad you did."

He grinned suddenly. "It may have been an idiotic reason, but I'm glad I did too."

They lay together peacefully, neither of them inclined to move. The room was almost in darkness when Anne suddenly jerked fully awake and said, "Good heavens, Daniel! It's time for dinner. We had better get dressed." She began to push the covers off of them.

"I like you better this way," he said, his eyes going over her naked body.

She smiled and said in a scolding voice, "There's a time for everything under the sun, and now it is time for dinner. Aren't you hungry?"

Daniel sat up. "Actually, I'm starving." He sounded surprised. "I could eat an entire leg of mutton all by myself."

Anne put on her robe and went to ring for her maid. "You had better go into your dressing room Daniel. I don't think Nancy should see you like that."

He grinned at her, the little-boy grin she loved so much, and disappeared from her sight.

*

Daniel had been home a week when he told Anne he wanted to make a quick visit to the factory.

She said eagerly, "Bonny and I would like to go with you. We want to speak to the mothers about the new school."

They were sitting at the breakfast table with Miss Bonteen, and Anne shot a quick look at her friend before saying, "We've worked out a course of study, figured out the size of the building and what the children will need. Both of us are very pleased with it. We think it will be a model for other village schools to follow."

Daniel looked from his wife to her friend, then back to his wife again. Her face was alight with enthusiasm. He wished she didn't want to do this. He didn't want her near the factory. He wanted her to remain at home, where she would be safe. But what right had he to tell Anne what she could and couldn't do? Yes, she had promised to serve and obey him, but she wasn't his servant. She wasn't just someone who kept the house and allowed him to have sex with her. She was the person he loved most in the world. Without her he would be alone again, and that he couldn't bear. He took a deep breath and said firmly, "That would be fine."

Her smile was his reward.

"What are these plans?" he asked.

They outlined their basic ideas and he was very impressed. "I wish I had an education like that," he said when Anne and Miss Bonteen finished. "But this plan will only work if there is someone on-site who can oversee it. An education supervisor of some sort."

"Bonny has volunteered to be the Head Mistress," Anne told him proudly.

Daniel looked at Miss Bonteen in surprise. "You're leaving us? But what will Anne do without you?"

Miss Bonteen gave Anne a misty smile before answering, "We have spoken about that, Mr. Dereham, and both of us believe that at this moment the factory children need me more than Anne does."

Daniel looked from Miss Bonteen, to his wife's smiling face and nodded his approval. "If that is what you both want, then that is what you shall have." He looked back to Miss Bonteen and said, "I always thought you would be here to teach our children."

He saw the tears spring to her eyes, and she sniffed. "Thank you. I promise that by the time your first child is ready to be taught, I will have that school running like clockwork. Then, if you wish me to return, I shall be happy to do so."

"You will always be welcome in this house, Bonny," Daniel said, using Anne's sobriquet for the first time. "Grex is your home as much as it is ours."

At that the tears spilled over, and Miss Bonteen excused herself and left the room, handkerchief in hand.

Daniel turned to Anne and found that she too had tears in her eyes. "Thank you," she said in a trembling voice. "Thank you for that, Daniel."

She started to search for a handkerchief, couldn't find one, took the napkin Daniel handed her and wiped her eyes. When she had finished, he said, "Anne, I have something I want to ask you."

She tilted her head a little. "What is it?"

He looked down at the shining wood of the table and took a long breath. He looked up again and said, "Will you come with me on a visit to my mother?"

Her face broke into a radiant smile. "Oh Daniel. I should love to come with you. I'm so glad you decided to do this. I know she will be happy to see you."

He looked down again. "I haven't been a good son, Annie. I blamed her, you see. I blamed her for lying to me, for making me believe I was someone other than who I was. I wasn't thinking very clearly when I jumped on that ship, and I don't think I've thought clearly about her ever since." He looked up and met her eyes. "I loved her very much. I loved her and I blamed her and I ran away from her. I never gave her a chance to explain. And my father—I know Owen Dereham is my real father, not the man who rejected me. I was so awful to him when he came to visit, Annie. I cringe when I think back on how awful I was."

179

"I'm sure he understood," she said.

"Do you think he'll hate me for rejecting him like that?"

She smiled, rose, came around the back of his chair and drew his head against her breast. "I think they will both be ecstatic to see you. Why don't you write a note to your mother this morning and set a date?"

"You don't think it would be better if we just arrived without notice? Suppose she writes back and says she doesn't want to see me?"

"That won't happen." The certainty in her voice reassured him. "Write the letter and say you'll be there next Sunday."

"But that will hardly give her time to write back and refuse to see me. I don't want to go there if..."

"Daniel," Anne said firmly. "Your mother will want to see you. Just write the letter and we'll set off early Sunday morning."

He lifted his head from her breast and looked up into her face. "Thank you," he said. "Thank you, my love. I was an empty shell of a man until I met you."

She bent her head to drop a kiss on his hair and the butler came into the room to remove the breakfast.

CHAPTER TWENTY-SEVEN

August 18, 1818

It was Owen Robert Daniel Dereham's first birthday and his grandparents were at Grex to help him celebrate. The weather was cooperating, and a lavish picnic had been spread on the newly built stone patio that opened off the new garden room. Both Owen's godparents were in attendance as well, and a few family friends from the parish had also been invited. Anne's father, Lord Grex, had recently died, and she and Daniel had been forced to cancel the more elaborate celebration they had initially planned.

The center of the festivities was sleeping on his grandmother's lap as she and his mother chatted comfortably under the shade of an awning. Dorothy was curled up at Anne's feet keeping an eye out for whatever food might drop to the floor.

"He must be getting heavy for you, Mother," Anne said. "Give him to me."

"He's not heavy at all," Maria Dereham protested. "You have him all the time, Anne. I need to take every chance I can to be close to him."

"If you and Father would only move in with us, as we are always urging you to do, you could see him all the time."

Maria smiled. There were lines in her forehead and around her mouth, but nothing could disguise the perfect bone structure of her face. She had given that bone structure to her son, who had in turn passed it along to her grandson.

Anne saw Miss Bonteen come out onto the patio and waved to her. As she came toward them, Lady Lovejoy, the squire's wife, stopped her, and she bent to listen to what that lady had to say.

Maria asked, "How is the school coming along?"

"Wonderfully. When the children first started they were a bit boisterous and disobedient, but Bonny took care of that very quickly. Whenever I've gone there now they are attentive and eager to learn. It's lovely to see."

Dorothy got up and trotted toward the man who was now approaching. She had fallen in love with Owen Dereham and Anne often humorously complained that she had been supplanted.

Owen smiled at his wife as he came up to them. "You look beautiful sitting there with a baby at your breast," he said.

"I could hold him forever," she returned.

"I was just telling Mother that if you came to live with us she could spend as much time as she liked with Owen," Anne said sweetly.

He laughed and took a seat next to his wife. "What would I do with myself all day if I lived here, lass? Have ye thought of that?"

"Yes," Anne returned promptly. "Daniel wants to restore the farms that my father let go derelict. Then he wants to get new tenants in. You'd be just the person to do that for him. You know a lot more about farming than he does."

Owen raised an interested eyebrow. "I did not know he planned to restore the farms."

"I know he wanted to speak to you about it. He probably hasn't had time yet."

Maria said, "That would certainly keep you busy, my dear. And you would be a help to Daniel as well."

Anne's attention diverted to the French doors that led from the house out to the patio. They were opening, and Daniel and Matthew stepped out on the patio. Matthew was Owen's godfather and, despite her protests that she was too old, Miss Bonteen had proudly become Owen's godmother.

The rector's wife said something to Daniel and he moved to join the group at her table. After Daniel had given the rector the money to put a new roof on the church, he and his wife regarded the owner of Grex as an angel sent by the Almighty. To his credit, Daniel appreciated the deep, fundamental goodness of the two elderly people and always made time for them.

Matthew came over to join Anne. She smiled up at him and said, "We appreciate your coming, Matthew. We truly didn't expect you to."

He laughed and sat down beside her. "I wouldn't miss my godson's first birthday for the world."

"How are Charlotte and Thomas doing?"

"Well enough. She's increasing again and is quite uncomfortable."

"Yes, so she wrote."

The entire Preston family was also in mourning. The earl had taken a fall at the end of the last hunting season and three days later had died. Matthew was now the Earl of Preston, and Daniel had been helping him sort out the assets and debits of Preston's stud farm.

The baby awoke suddenly and began to cry. Maria tried to rock him but he fought her. "I give up," she said to Anne. "He's too big for me."

"He's getting teeth and he's been miserable," Anne said, getting up. "We're lucky he was quiet for so long." She lifted Owen Robert Daniel from his grandmother's lap and kissed his head. "There, there, little one. We'll go inside and see if there's something you want to eat."

"Walk," her son demanded. He squirmed in her embrace. "Walk, Walk, Walk!" He had begun to walk when he was ten months old and no longer wanted to be carried.

"All right. But we're going back into the house." Anne put him down and took his hand. "Ready?"

"Yes."

Maria watched misty-eyed as Anne and the baby walked slowly toward the house. "She's such a wonderful mother," she said.

"Won't you sit down, Lord Preston," Owen said.

Matthew took Anne's empty seat. "I don't think my godson's grandparents should be calling his godfather by his title. Please, won't you call me Matthew?"

He was looking at Maria as he spoke, and she flushed and dropped her eyes. They were both cognizant of the wrong his father had done to her and it still made for some awkwardness between them. She had not expressed regret for his father's death, and he hadn't expected her to.

Owen asked him a question about the geological map he had been working on with William Smith and soon the two men were immersed in talk about rocks and fossils and dates. Maria listened to them, a faint smile on her face. After meeting Matthew at the baby's christening, Owen had developed a keen interest in geology. They were deep in discussion when Daniel joined them.

"Thank heavens," Maria said. "A human being who is not obsessed by rocks."

Daniel grinned and the two men hastened to apologize to Maria. She smiled and said, "I was only joking. I think it's wonderful that Owen has discovered this interest." She patted the seat next to her and said to her son, "Sit down and talk to me, Daniel. I haven't had you to myself since we arrived."

Daniel obeyed with alacrity and the rest of the afternoon passed pleasantly for all his guests.

*

Daniel didn't come up to bed until after midnight, and he was surprised to find Anne still awake. She was sitting up in bed reading a book by the light of the gas lamp on the table next to her. She put it down on her lap when he came in.

"Still awake?" he said as he came toward her.

He was still immaculately dressed in dinner attire, and his blue eyes looked crystal clear as he sat next to her on the bed. She said with surprise, "You haven't been drinking?"

"No." He lifted his eyebrows. "Did you expect me to totter in here drunk?"

She smiled. "No, but I thought you and Matthew and Owen might be sharing a bottle or two."

"Believe it or not, we have been talking about geology," he said. "Matthew was telling us about the fossils Smith has been finding embedded in the different strata of rocks and how they can be used to match rocks across different regions of the country."

"I know your father is fascinated by this science. I didn't know you shared his interest."

He sat on her side of the bed. "I don't really. I was watching my father. He's done a lot of reading on the subject and he asked Matthew some highly intelligent questions. I could see Matthew was impressed."

She reached up and began to unfasten his tie. "If Owen had been born to wealthy parents he would have gone to university where he could have studied about rocks."

"He was the one who made me go to the village school. All the other farmers' sons had to work on their fathers' farms, but Owen made me go to school."

"He was a wonderful father," Anne said.

"He was the best."

Anne was now working on his shirt, pulling it out of his trousers and beginning to open it. He didn't say a word, just sat and let her do it.

"Did you speak to him about taking over the farms?" she asked.

"Yes. I also told him Matthew says there are some interesting rock formations right here at Grex he might like to take a look at."

"Clever," she said admiringly.

He stood up and began to unfasten his trousers. "Good thing I told Lloyd not to wait up for me, that I could undress myself tonight. I never thought to get help from my wife."

Anne smiled serenely. "I feel happy."

"Good." He came over to the bed and got in next to her, leaning up on his elbow.

She looked up at the dark angel that was her husband and whispered, "Kiss me."

He did.

About the Author

Joan Wolf is a *USA TODAY* bestselling author whose highly reviewed books include some forty novels set in the period of the English Regency. She fell in love with the Regency when she was a young girl and discovered the novels of Georgette Heyer. Although she has strayed from the period now and then, it has always remained her favorite.

Joan was born and brought up in New York City but has spent most of her adult life with her husband and two children in Connecticut. She has a passion for animals and over the years has filled the house with a variety of much-loved dogs and cats. Her great love for her horses has spilled over into every book she has written. The total number of her published novels is fifty-three and she has no plans to retire.

"Joan Wolf never fails to deliver the best."
—Nora Roberts

"Joan Wolf is absolutely wonderful. I've loved her work for years."
—Iris Johansen

"As a writer, she's an absolute treasure."
—Linda Howard

"Strong, compelling fiction."
—Amanda Quick

"Joan Wolf writes with an absolute emotional mastery that goes straight to the heart."
—Mary Jo Putney

"Wolf's Regency historicals are as delicious and addictive as dark, rich, Belgian chocolates."
—Publishers Weekly

"Joan Wolf is back in the Regency saddle—hallelujah!"
—Catherine Coulter

* * *

To sign up for Joan's newsletter, email her at
joanemwolf@gmail.com.

CPSIA information can be obtained
at www.ICGtesting.com
Printed in the USA
LVHW090959130520
655427LV00001BA/136